THE
CONSEQUENCES
OF THAT NIGHT

THE CONSEQUENCES OF THAT NIGHT

BY

JENNIE LUCAS

First published in Great Britain 2013
by Mills & Boon, an imprint of Harlequin (UK) Limited,
Large Print edition 2014
Eton House, 18-24 Paradise Road,
Richmond, Surrey, TW9 1SR

© 2013 Jennie Lucas

ISBN: 978 0 263 24028 3

Harlequin (UK) Limited's policy is to use papers that are natural, renewable and recyclable products and made from wood grown in sustainable forests. The logging and manufacturing processes conform to the legal environmental regulations of the country of origin.

Printed and bound in Great Britain
by CPI Antony Rowe, Chippenham, Wiltshire

CHAPTER ONE

A BABY.

Emma Hayes put a hand over her slightly curved belly, swaying as the double-decker bus traveled deeper into central London in the gray afternoon rain.

A baby.

For ten weeks, she'd tried not to hope. Tried not to think about it. Even when she'd gone to her doctor's office that morning, she'd been bracing herself for some problem, to be told that she must be brave.

Instead she'd seen a rapid steady beat on the sonogram as her doctor pointed to the flash on the screen. "See the heartbeat? 'Hi, Mum.'"

"I'm really pregnant?" she'd said through dry lips.

The man's eyes twinkled through his spectacles. "As pregnant as can be."

"And the baby's—all right?"

"It's all going perfectly. Textbook, I'd say." The doctor had given her a big smile. "I think it's safe to tell your husband now, Mrs. Hayes."

Her husband. The words echoed through Emma's mind as she closed her eyes, leaning back into her seat on the top deck of the Number 9 bus. Her husband. How she wished there was such a person, waiting for her in a homey little cottage—a man who'd kiss her with a cry of joy at the news of his coming child. But in direct opposition to what she'd told her physician, there was no husband.

Just a boss. A boss who'd made love to her nearly three months ago in a single night of reckless passion, then disappeared in the cold dawn, leaving her to wake up alone in his huge bed. The same bed that she'd made for him over the past seven years, complete with ironed sheets.

I know the maid could do it, but I prefer that you handle it personally. No one can do it like you, Miss Hayes.

Oh, boy. She'd really handled it personally this time, hadn't she?

Blinking, Emma stared out the window as the red double-decker bus made its way down

Kensington Road. Royal Albert Hall went by in a blur of red brick behind the rain-streaked glass. She wiped her eyes hard. Stupid tears. She shouldn't be crying. She was happy about this baby. Thrilled, in fact. She'd honestly thought she could never get pregnant. It was a miracle.

A lump rose in her throat.

Except...

Cesare would never be a real father to their baby. He would never be her husband, a man who would kiss her when he came home from work and tuck their baby in at night. No matter how she might wish otherwise.

Because Cesare Falconeri, self-made billionaire, sexy Italian playboy, had two passions in life. The first was expanding his far-flung hotel empire across the globe, working relentlessly to expand his net worth and power. The second, a mere hobby when he had an hour or two to spare, was to seduce beautiful women, which he did for sport, as other men might play football or golf.

Her sexy Italian boss annihilated the thin hearts of supermodels and heiresses alike with the same careless, seductive, selfish charm. He cared nothing for any of them. Emma knew that. As his housekeeper, she was the one responsible for arranging morning-after gifts for his one-night stands. Usually Cartier watches. Bought in bulk.

As the bus traveled through Mayfair, the lights of the Ritz Hotel slid by. Looking down from the top deck of the bus, Emma saw pedestrians dressed in Londoners' typical festive autumn attire—that is to say, entirely in black—struggling with umbrellas in the rain and wind.

It was the first of November. Just yesterday, the warmth of Indian summer had caressed the city like a lover, with promises of forever. Today, drizzle and rain had descended. The city, so recently bright and warm, had become melancholy, haunted and filled with despair.

Or maybe it was just her.

For the past seven years—since she'd first started as a maid at Cesare's hotel in New York, at the age of twenty-one—she'd been absolutely in love with him, and absolutely careful not to show it. Careful not to show any feelings at all.

You never bore me with personal stories, Miss Hayes. I hardly know anything about you. He'd smiled. *Thank you.*

Then three months ago, she'd come back from

her stepmother's funeral in Texas and he'd found her alone in his darkened kitchen, clutching an unopened bottle of tequila, with tears streaming down her cheeks. For a moment, Cesare had just stared at her.

Then he'd pulled her roughly into his arms.

Perhaps he'd only meant to offer comfort, but by the end of the night, he'd taken the virginity she'd saved for him, just for him, even when she knew she had no hope. He'd taken her to his bed, and made Emma's gray, lonely world explode with color and fire.

And today, a new magic, every bit as shocking and unexpected. She was pregnant with his baby.

Emma traced her fingertip into the shape of a heart against a fogged-up corner of the bus window. If only his playboy nature could change. If only she could believe he'd actually wish to be a father someday, and even fall in love with Emma, as she'd fallen for him…

The double-decker bus jolted to a stop, and with an intake of breath she abruptly wiped the heart off the glass. Cesare, *love?* That was a laugh. He couldn't even stick around for breakfast, much less commit to raising a family!

Ever since she'd woken up alone in his bed that cold morning after, Emma had faithfully kept his mansion in Kensington sparkling clean in perpetual hope for his arrival. But she'd found out from one of the secretaries that he'd actually returned to London two days ago. Instead of coming home, he was staying at his suite at the flagship London Falconeri near Trafalgar Square.

His unspoken words were clear. He wanted to make sure Emma knew she meant nothing to him, any more than the stream of models and starlets who routinely paraded through his bed.

But there was one big difference. None of his other lovers had gotten pregnant.

Because unlike the rest, he'd slept with her without protection. He'd believed her when she'd whispered to him in the dark that pregnancy was impossible. Cesare, who trusted no one, had taken Emma at her word.

Her hands tightened on the handrail of the seat in front of her. Here she'd been fantasizing about homey cottages and Cesare miraculously turning into a devoted father. The truth was that when he learned their one-night stand had caused a pregnancy, he'd think she'd lied. That she'd deliberately gotten pregnant to trap him.

He'd *hate* her.

So don't tell him, a cowardly voice whispered. *Run away. Take that job in Paris. He never has to know.*

But she couldn't keep her pregnancy a secret. Even if the odds were a million to one that he'd want to be part of their baby's life, didn't even Cesare deserve that chance?

A loud burst of laughter, and the stomp of people climbing to the top deck, made Emma glance out the window. She leaped to her feet. "Wait, please!" she cried to the bus driver, who obligingly waited as she ran down the bus stairs, nearly tripping over her own feet. Out on the sidewalk, buffeted by passersby, she looked up at the elegant, imposing gray-stone Falconeri Hotel. Putting her handbag over her head to dodge the rain, Emma ran into the grand lobby. Nodding at the security guard, she shook the rain off her camel-colored mackintosh and took the elevator to the tenth floor.

Trembling, she walked down the hall to the suite of rooms Cesare occasionally used as an office and a pied-à-terre after a late evening out in Covent Garden. Cesare liked to be in the thick of things. The floor wasn't private, but shared by those guests who could afford rooms at a thousand pounds a night. Trembling, she knocked on the door.

She heard a noise on the other side, and then the door was abruptly wrenched open.

Emma looked up with an intake of breath. "Cesare…"

But it wasn't her boss. Instead a gorgeous young woman, barely covered in lingerie, stood in his doorway.

"Yes?" the woman said in a bored tone, leaning against the door as if she owned it.

A blade of ice went through Emma's heart as she recognized the woman. Olga Lukin. The famous model who had dated Cesare last year. Her body shook as she tried to say normally, "Is Mr. Falconeri here?"

"Who are you?"

"His—his housekeeper."

"Oh." The supermodel's shoulders relaxed. "He's in the shower."

"The shower," Emma repeated numbly.

"Yesss," Olga Lukin said with exaggerated slowness. "Do you want me to give him a message?"

"Um…"

"There's no point in you waiting." The blonde glanced back at the mussed bed, plainly visible in the hotel suite, and gave a catlike smile. "As soon as he's done, we're going out." Leaning forward, she confided in a stage whisper, "Right after we have another go."

Emma looked at Olga's bony shape, her cheekbones that could cut glass. She was absolutely gorgeous, a woman who'd look perfect on any billionaire's arm. *In his bed.*

While Emma—she suddenly felt like nothing. Nobody. Short, round and drab, not particularly pretty, with the big hips of someone who loved extra cookies at teatime, wearing a beige raincoat, knit dress and sensible shoes. Her long black hair, when it wasn't pulled back in a plaited chignon, hadn't seen the inside of a hairdresser's in years.

Humiliation made her ears burn. How could she have dreamed, even for an instant, that Cesare might want to marry someone like her and raise a baby in a snug little cottage?

He must have slept with her that night out of *pity*—nothing more!

"Well?"

"No." Emma shook her head, hiding her tears. "No message."

"Ta, then," she said rudely. But as she started to close the door, there was a loud bang as Cesare came out of the bathroom.

Emma's heart stopped in her chest as she saw him for the first time since he'd left her in his bed.

Cesare was nearly naked, wearing only a low-slung white towel around his hips, gripping another towel wrapped carelessly over his broad shoulders. His tanned, muscular chest was bare, his black hair still damp from the shower. He stopped, scowling at Olga.

"What are you—"

Then he saw Emma in the doorway, and his spine snapped straight. His darkly handsome face turned blank. "Miss Hayes."

Miss Hayes? He was back to calling her that—

when for the past five years they'd been on a first-name basis? *Miss Hayes?*

After so long of hiding her every emotion from him, purely out of self-preservation, something cracked in her heart. She looked from him, to Olga, to the mussed bed.

"Is this your way of showing me my place?" She shook her head tearfully. "What is *wrong* with you, Cesare?"

His dark eyes widened in shock.

Staggering back, horrified at what she'd said, and brokenhearted at what she'd not been able to say, she turned and fled.

"Miss Hayes," she heard him call behind her, and then, "Emma!"

She kept going. Her throat throbbed with pain. She ran with all her heart, desperate to reach the safety of the elevator, where she could burst into tears in privacy. And start planning an immediate departure for Paris, where she'd never have to face him again—or remember her own foolish dreams.

A father for her baby. A snug home. A happy family. A man who'd love her back, who would protect her, who'd be faithful. A tear fell for each crushed dream. She wiped her eyes furiously. How could she have ever let herself get in this position—with Cesare, of all people? Why hadn't she been more careful? *Why?*

Emma heard his low, rough curse behind her, and the hard thud of his bare feet. Before she reached the elevator, he grabbed her arm, whirling her around in the hall.

"What do you want, Miss Hayes?" he demanded.

"Miss Hayes?" she bit out, struggling to get free. "Are you kidding me with that? We've seen each other naked!"

He released her, clearly surprised by her sharp tone.

"That doesn't explain what you're doing here," he said stiffly. "You've never sought me out like this before."

No, and she never would again! "Sorry I interrupted your date."

"It's not a— I have no idea what Olga is doing in my room. She must have gotten a key and snuck in."

Hot tears burned behind her eyes. "Right."

"We broke up months ago."

"Looks like you're back together."

"Not so far as I'm concerned."

"Now, that I believe," she choked out. "Because once you have sex, any relationship is pretty much over where you're concerned, isn't it?"

"We didn't just have sex." He set his jaw. "Have you ever known me to lie?"

That stopped her.

"No," she whispered. Cesare never lied. He always made his position brutally clear. No commitment, no promises, no future.

Yet, somehow many women still managed to convince themselves otherwise. To believe they were special. Until they woke alone the morning after, to find Emma serving them breakfast with their going-away present, and ended up weeping in her arms.

"I really don't care." Emma ran an unsteady hand over her forehead. "It's none of my business."

"No. It's not."

She took a deep breath. "I just came to…to tell you something."

The dim lighting of the elegant hotel hallway left hard shadows against Cesare's cheekbones, the dark scruff of his jaw, and his muscular, tanned chest. His black eyes turned grim. "Don't."

Her lips parted on an intake of breath. "What?"

"Just don't."

"You don't even know what I'm going to say."

"I can guess. You're going to tell me all about your feelings. You've always shared so little. I convinced myself you didn't have any. That I was just a job to you."

Emma almost laughed hysterically in his face. Oh, if only he knew. For years, she'd worked for him until her brain was numb and her fingers were about to fall off. Her first thought each morning when she woke—was him. Her last thought before she finally collapsed in bed each night—was him. What he needed. What he wanted. What he would need and want tomorrow. He'd always been more than a job to her.

"It kept things simple," he said. "It's why we got along so well. I liked you. Respected you. I'd started to think of us as—friends."

Friends. Against her will, Emma's gaze fell to the hard planes of his muscular, tanned chest laced with dark hair. Wearing only the low-slung white towel wrapped snugly around his hips, he was six feet three inches of powerful, hard-muscled masculinity, and he stood in the hallway of his hotel without the slightest self-consciousness, as arrogant as if he were wearing a tailored suit. A few people passed them in the hallway, openly staring. Emma swallowed. It would be hard for any woman to resist staring at Cesare. Even now she… God help her, even now…

"Now you're going to ruin it." His eyes became flinty. "You're going to tell me that you *care*. You've rushed down here to explain you still can't forget our night together. Even though we both swore it wouldn't change anything, you're going to tell me you're desperately in love with me." He scowled. "I thought you were special, but you're going to prove you're just like the rest."

The reverberations of his cruel words echoed in the empty hallway, like a bullet ricocheting against the walls before it landed square and deep in her heart.

For a moment, Emma couldn't breathe. Then she forced herself to meet his eyes.

"I would have to be stupid to love you," she

said in a low voice. "I know you too well. You'll never love anyone, ever again."

He blinked. "So you're not—in love with me?"

He sounded so hopeful. She stared up at him, her heart pounding, tears burning behind her eyes. "I'd have to be the biggest idiot who ever lived."

His dark gaze softened. "I don't want to lose you, Emma. You're irreplaceable."

"I am?"

He gave a single nod. "You are the only one who knows how to properly make my bed. Who can maintain my home in perfect order. I need you."

The bullet went a little deeper into her heart.

"Oh," she whispered, and it was the sound someone makes when they've been punched in the belly. He wanted to keep her *as his employee.* She was irreplaceable in his life—*as his employee.*

Three months ago, when he'd taken her in his arms and kissed her passionately, her whole world had changed forever. But for Cesare, nothing had changed. He still expected her to be his invisible, replaceable servant who had no feelings and existed solely to serve his needs.

Tell me this won't change anything between us, he'd said in the darkness that night.

I promise, she'd breathed.

But it was a promise she couldn't keep. Not when she was pregnant with his baby. After so many years of keeping her feelings buried deep inside, she couldn't do it anymore. Maybe it was the pregnancy hormones, or maybe the anguish of hope. But emotions were suddenly bleeding out of her that she couldn't control. Grief and heartbreak and something new.

Anger.

"So that was why you ran away from me three months ago?" she said. "Because you were terrified that if I actually woke up in your arms, I'd fall desperately in love with you?"

Cesare looked irritated. "I didn't exactly run away—"

"I woke up alone," she said unsteadily. She ran her trembling hand back through the dark braids of her chignon. "You regretted sleeping with me."

He set his jaw. "If I'd known you were a virgin..." He exhaled, looking down the gilded hallway with a flare of nostril before he turned back to her. "It never should have happened. But you knew the score. I stayed away these past months to give us both some space to get past it."

"You mean, pretend it never happened."

"There's no reason to let a single reckless night ruin a solid arrangement." He folded his arms over his bare chest, over the warm skin that she'd once stroked and felt sliding against her own naked body in the dark hush of night. "You are the best housekeeper I've ever had. I want to keep it that way. That night meant nothing to either of us. You were sad, and I was trying to comfort you. That's all."

It was the final straw.

"I see," she bit out. "So I should just go back to folding your socks and keeping your home tidy, and if I remember the night you took my virginity at all, I should be grateful you were such a kind employer—comforting me in my hour of need. You are truly too good to me, Mr. Falconeri."

He frowned, sensing sarcasm. "Um…"

"Thank you for taking pity on me that night. It must have felt like quite a sacrifice, seducing me to make the crying stop. Thank you for your compassion."

Cesare glared at her, looking equal parts shocked and furious. "You've never spoken like this before. What the hell's gotten into you, Emma?"

Your baby, she wanted to say. *But you don't even care you took my virginity. You just want me back to cook and clean for you.* Anger flashed through her. "For God's sake, don't you think I have any feelings at all?"

He clenched his hands at his sides, then exhaled.

"No," he said quietly. "I hoped you didn't."

The lump in her throat felt like a razorblade now.

"Well. Sorry. I'm not a robot. No matter how inconvenient that is for you." She fought the rush of tears. "Everything has changed for me now."

"Nothing changed for me."

Emma lifted her gaze to his. "It could, if you'd just give it a chance." She hated the pleading sound of her voice. "If you'd only just listen…"

Cesare's eyes were already hardening, his sensual lips parting to argue, when they heard a gasp. Emma turned to see an elderly couple staring at them in the hotel hallway. The white-haired man looked scandalized at the sight of Cesare wearing only a white towel, while his wife peered at him through her owlish glasses with interest.

Cesare glared at them. "Do you mind?" he said coldly. "We are trying to have a private conversation."

The man looked nonplussed. "I beg your pardon." He fled toward the elevator, pulling his wife with him, though she shot Cesare's backside one last look of appreciative regret.

He turned back to Emma with a scowl. "Nothing can change for me. Don't you understand?"

It already had. He just didn't know it. Emma swallowed. She'd never thought she'd be forced to blurt out news of her pregnancy in the middle of a public hotel hallway. She licked her lips. "Look, can't we go somewhere? Talk about this in private?"

"Why? So you can confess your undying love?" His voice was full of scorn. "So you can tell me how you'll be the woman to make me love again? How you've imagined me proposing to you? How you've dreamed of standing next to me in a white dress?"

"It's not like that," she tried, but he'd seen her flinch. It was exactly like that.

"Damn you, Emma," he said softly. "You are the one woman who should have known better. I will not change, not for you or anyone. All you've succeeded in doing with this stunt is destroying our friendship. I don't see how we can continue to maintain a working relationship after this...."

"Do you think I'll even *want* to be your house-keeper after this?"

His eyes widened, then narrowed.

"So much for promises," he bit out.

She flinched again, wondering what he would say when she told him about the far worse promise she'd unknowingly broken—the one about it being impossible for her to get pregnant.

But how could she tell him? How could she blurt out the precious news of their child, standing in a public hallway with him staring at her as if he despised her? If only they could just go back to his room—but no. His suite was already filled, with a hard-eyed blonde in skimpy lingerie.

Everything suddenly became clear.

There was no room for a baby in Cesare's life. And Emma's only place there, as far as he was concerned, was scrubbing his floor and folding his sheets.

Cesare's expression was irritated. "If things can't be like they were…"

"What? You'll fire me for caring? That's your big threat?" Looking at the darkly handsome, arrogant face that she'd loved for so long, fury overwhelmed her. Fury at her own stupidity that she'd wasted so much of her life loving a man who couldn't see a miracle when it was right in front of him. Who wouldn't want the miracle, even if he did see.

How could she have loved him? How could she have ever thought—just as he'd accused her—that she could change his playboy nature?

He exhaled, and moderated his tone in a visible effort. "What if I offered to double your salary?"

Her lips parted in shock. "You want to *pay* me for our night together?"

"No," he said coldly. "I want to pay you to forget."

Her eyes stung. Of course he would offer *money*.

It was just paper to him, like confetti. One of his weapons, along with his power and masculine beauty, that he used to get his way. And Cesare Falconeri always got his way.

Emma shook her head.

"So how can we get past this? What the hell do you want from me?"

She looked up at him, her heart full of grief. What did she want? A man who loved her, who would love their child, who would be protective and loyal and show up for breakfast every morning. She whispered, "I want more than you will ever be able to give."

He knew immediately she wasn't speaking of money. That was clear by the way his handsome face turned grim, almost haunted in the dim light of the hallway. He took a step toward her. "Emma…"

"Forget it." She stepped back. Her whole body was shaking. If he touched her now, if he said anything more to remind her what a fool she'd been, she was afraid she'd collapse into sobs on the carpet and never get up again.

Her baby needed her to be strong. Starting now.

Down the hall, she heard the elevator ding.

Glancing back, she saw the elderly couple hesitate in front of the elevator, obviously still watching them. She realized they'd been listening to every word. Turning back to Cesare, she choked out, "I'm done being your slave."

"You tell him, honey," the white-haired woman called approvingly.

Cesare's expression turned to cold fury, but Emma didn't wait. She just ran for the elevator. She got her arm between the doors in time to step inside, next to the elderly couple. Trembling, she turned back to face the man she'd loved for seven years. The boss whose baby she now carried, though he did not know it.

Cesare was stalking toward her, his almost-naked body muscular and magnificent in the hallway of his own billion-dollar hotel.

"Come back," he ground out, his dark eyes flashing. "I'm not done talking to you."

Now, that was funny. In a tragic, heart-wrenching, want-to-burst-into-sobs kind of way. "I tried to talk to you. You wouldn't let me. You were too terrified I'd say those three fatal words." She gave a bitter laugh. "So here are two words for

you instead." Emma lifted glittering eyes to his.
"I quit."

And the elevator doors closed between them.

CHAPTER TWO

I'M DONE BEING your slave.

Cesare's body was taut with fury as the elevator doors closed in front of Emma's defiant, beautiful face. He could still hear the echo of her scornful words.

I want more than you will ever be able to give.

And then she'd quit.

Cesare couldn't believe it.

It was true that in the past few months, he'd thought once or twice about firing Emma rather than face her again. But he'd promised himself he wouldn't fire her. As long as she didn't get silly or ask for a *relationship*. After all they'd been through together, he didn't want to lose her.

He'd never expected this. He was the one who left women. They didn't leave *him*. Not since…

He cut off the thought.

Turning, he stalked back down the hall, passing a wealthy hotel guest, a heavily bejeweled white-haired lady dressed in vintage Chanel, holding a small Pomeranian in her arms. An entourage of three servants trailed behind her. She glared at him.

Ah. Cesare's lip curled in a mixture of admiration and scorn. The wealthy. He hated them all sometimes. Even though he himself had somehow become one of them.

Returning to his suite, he realized he had no key. And he was still wearing only a towel. At any moment someone would snap an embarrassing photograph, to add to the rest of his indiscretions already permanently emblazoned all over the internet. Irritated, he pounded on his own door with the flat of his hand.

Olga opened the door, still in her lingerie, holding a lit cigarette.

"There's no smoking in this hotel," he snapped, walking past her. "Put that out."

She took a long puff, then snuffed it out in the bottom of a water glass. "Problems with your housekeeping staff?" she asked sweetly.

"How did you get in here?"

"You sound as if you're not glad to see me." Pouting, Olga slinked forward, swaying her hips in a way that was no doubt supposed to be enticing. He almost wished it were. If he'd still been attracted to her, maybe he wouldn't have made such a mess of things with Emma. Because he couldn't go back to thinking of Emma Hayes just as an employee, no matter how he wished he could. Not when every time he closed his eyes, he remembered the way she'd felt beneath him in the hot breathless hush of night.

Don't worry. I can't get pregnant, she'd whispered, putting her hand over his as he'd reached for a condom in his bedside stand. *It's impossible. I promise you...*

And he'd believed her. Emma Hayes was the first, and only, woman he'd ever slept with without a condom. In his whole life.

The way it had felt—the way *she* had felt…

Cesare ground his teeth. His plan of dealing with the aftermath had not gone well. After three months apart, he'd convinced himself that surely, cool, sensible, emotionless Emma had forgotten their night together.

But she hadn't. And neither had he.

Damn it.

"You haven't been photographed with any other

women for ages," Olga purred. "I knew that could only mean one thing. You've missed me, as I've missed you."

Looking up, Cesare blinked. He'd forgotten she was there.

She gave him a sultry smile. "We were good together, weren't we?"

"No." Cesare stared at her. "We weren't." Picking up the designer clothes and expensive leather boots she'd left in a neat stack by the bed, he held them out to her. "Please get out." In his current frame of mind, he was impressed with himself for managing the *please.*

Olga frowned, licking her red, bee-stung lips. "Are you kidding?"

"No."

"But—you can't send me away. I'm still in love with you!"

Cesare rolled his eyes. "Let me guess. You're having some sort of crisis because your bookings are down. You're ready to give up the difficulties of the modeling business and settle down, marry rich, have a child or two before you devote the rest of your life to shopping for jewels and furs."

Her cheeks turned red, and he knew he was

right. It would have been funny, but this had happened too often for him to find it amusing anymore.

Her long lashes fluttered. "No one understands you like I do, Cesare. No one will ever love you like I do!"

Crossing the suite, he opened the door, and tossed her clothes and boots into the hallway.

"Cara," he drawled, "you're breaking my heart."

Olga's eyes changed from pleading to anger in a moment, leaving him to feel reasonably assured that her so-called love was worth exactly what the sentiment usually was: nothing, a breath of wind, once spoken, instantly lost.

"You'll be sorry!" She stomped past him, then stopped outside the doorway, wiggling her nearly-bare bottom at him. "You'll never have all *this* ever again!"

"Tragic," he said coldly, and closed the door.

His suite went quiet. Cesare stood for a moment, unmoving. He felt weary as the emotion of the past hour came crashing around him.

Emma. He'd lost her. She'd acted like all the other women, so he'd treated her like one.

The trouble was that she was different.

Maybe it's for the best, he thought. Things had gone too far between them. It had become… dangerous. Scowling, he dropped his towel and pulled a black shirt and pants from his wardrobe. The pants were slightly wrinkled, and the shirt had been oddly ironed. They didn't even have the right smell, because Emma hadn't been the one to wash, dry and fold them.

But it wasn't her laundry skills he missed most. He looked out the window. The lights of London's theater district were already twinkling in the dusk.

Cesare had always liked the environment of hotels, the way the faces of the people changed, the sameness of the rooms, the way a man could easily move out of one hotel and change to the next without anyone questioning his constancy, or thinking there was a flaw in his soul.

He'd known Emma Hayes's value since she'd first joined the housekeeping staff of his hotel on Park Avenue in New York. She'd been in charge of the penthouse floor, where he stayed while in the city, and he'd been so impressed by her work ethic and meticulous skills that she'd become assistant head housekeeper within the first year, and then head housekeeper when he'd opened the Falconeri in London. Now, she supervised the staff of his Kensington mansion. Taking care of him exclusively.

But she didn't just keep Cesare in clean socks. She kept him in line. Unlike other employees, unlike even his friends, Emma wasn't overly impressed by him. She'd become his sounding board. Almost like…family.

How could he have let himself seduce her? He needed her. He could always count on Emma. She always put his needs first. She never even asked for time off. Not until three months ago, when she'd abruptly left for a long weekend.

The Kensington house had felt strangely empty without her. He'd avoided coming home. On the third night, he'd returned from an unsatisfactory date at two in the morning, expecting to find a silent, dark house. Instead, he'd heard a noise from the kitchen and felt a flash of pleasure when he realized Emma must have returned early.

He'd found her sitting alone in the dark kitchen, holding a tequila bottle. Her black dress was wrinkled. Her eyes had dark smudges beneath them, as if she'd been crying, and her long black hair was unkempt, cascading thickly down her shoulders.

"Emma?" he'd said, hardly believing his eyes. "Are you all right?"

"I just came back from Texas," she whispered, not looking at him. "From a funeral."

He'd never seen her drink before, he realized—not so much as a glass of champagne. "I'm sorry," he said uncomfortably, edging closer. He didn't know anything about her family. "Was it someone you loved?"

She shook her head. "My stepmother." Her fingers clutched compulsively around the bottle. He saw it was still unopened. "For years, I sent money to pay her bills. But it never changed her opinion. Marion always said I was selfish, a ruiner of lives. That I'd never amount to anything." She drew in a shaking breath. "And she was right."

"What are you talking about?" he said, taking an instant dislike to this Marion person, dead though she might be.

Emma flung an unsteady arm around to indicate the immaculate, modern kitchen. "Just look."

Cesare looked around, then turned back. "It's perfect," he said quietly. "Because you're the best at what you do."

"Cleaning up other people's lives," she'd said bitterly. "Being the perfect servant. Invisible like a ghost."

He'd never heard her voice like that, angry and full of self-recrimination. "Emma..."

"I thought she'd forgive me in the end." Her voice was muffled as she sagged in the kitchen stool, covering her face with a trembling hand. "But she left me no message in her will. Not her blessing. Not her forgiveness. Nothing."

"Forgiveness—for what?"

She looked at him for a long moment, then she turned her face toward the shadows without answering. She took a deep breath. "Now I'm truly alone."

Something had twisted in Cesare's chest. An answering pain in his own scarred heart, long buried but never completely healed. Going to her, he'd taken the bottle from her hand. He'd set it on the kitchen counter. Reaching out, he'd cupped her cheek.

"You're not alone." His eyes had fallen to her trembling pink lips as he breathed, "Emma…"

And then…

He'd only meant to offer solace, but somehow, he still wasn't sure how, things had spiraled out of control. He remembered the taste of her lips when he'd first kissed her. The look in her deep, warm green eyes as he covered her naked body with his own. The shock and reverence that had gone through him when he realized he was her very first lover.

She was totally different from any woman he'd taken to his bed before. It wasn't just the alluring warmth of her makeup-free face, or her total lack of artifice, or the long, dark hair pulled back in an old-fashioned chignon. It wasn't just her body's soft plump curves, so different from the starvation regime demanded by starlets and models these days.

It was the fact that he actually respected her.

He actually—liked her.

Everything about Emma, and the way she served him without criticism or demand, was comfort. Magic. *Home.*

But if he'd known she was a virgin, he never would have—

Yes, you would, he snarled at himself, remembering the tremble of her soft, tender lips beneath his, the salt of tears on her skin that night. The way she'd felt to him that night…the way she'd made him feel…

Cesare shook his head savagely. Whatever the pleasure, the cost was too high. Waking up the next morning, he'd realized the scope of his mistake. Because there was only one way his love affairs ended. With an awkward kiss-off, a bouquet of roses and an expensive gold watch, handed over by his one indispensable person—Emma herself.

He clawed back his short dark hair, still damp from his shower. His jaw was tight as he remembered the stricken expression on her pale, lovely face when she'd seen Olga in lingerie, standing in front of a bed which had been mussed, not with lovemaking, but from his hopeless attempt at sleep after a night on the phone with the Asia office. Of course Emma wouldn't know that, but why should he be obligated to explain?

What is wrong with you, Cesare?

Nothing was wrong with him, he thought grimly. It was the rest of the world that was screwed up, with stupid promises and rose-colored illusions. With people who pretended words like *love* and *forever* were more than sentiments on a Valentine's Day card.

He'd told himself Emma had no feelings for him, that their night together had been just an escape from grief. It meant nothing. He'd told himself that again and again. Told himself that if Emma tried to call it love, he'd break in a new housekeeper—even if that meant replacing her with someone who'd have the audacity to expect tea breaks and four weeks off every August.

But he'd never expected that Emma herself would just walk away.

Cesare looked out into the deepening autumn night. She'd done him a favor, really. She couldn't be his friend *and* his lover *and* know all his household secrets. It was too much. It left him too—vulnerable.

You are truly too good to me, Mr. Falconeri.

Cesare rubbed the back of his neck. He didn't deserve that. He *had* been a good employer to Emma. Hadn't he done everything a boss could do—paying her well, respecting her opinion, giving her independence to run his home? For the past few years, as they'd grown closer, he'd resisted an inconvenient desire for her. He wasn't used to ignoring temptation, but he'd done it, at least until three months ago. And as for what had happened that night...virgin or no—the way she'd licked her full pink lips and looked up at him with those heartbreaking eyes, how could he resist that? *Christo santo,* he was only a man.

But for that momentary weakness, she was now punishing him. Abandoning him without so much as a by-your-leave.

Fine. He growled under his breath. Let her quit. He didn't give a damn. His hands tightened. He *didn't.*

Except...

He did.

Cursing himself, he started for the door.

Emma wearily climbed out of the Tube station at Kensington High Street. Making her way through crowds of early evening commuters, she wiped rain from her cheek. It had to be rain. She couldn't be crying over Cesare.

So he'd never given her a chance to tell him he was going to be a father. So she'd found him in a hotel room with his ex-girlfriend, the lingerie model. So Emma was now all alone, with a baby to raise and nothing to help her but the memory of broken dreams.

She was going to be fine.

She exhaled, shifting her aching shoulders. She'd phone Alain Bouchard and accept that job in Paris. He'd give her decent hours, along with a good paycheck. She needed to be more sensible, now that she'd soon be a single mother.

Passing a shop selling Cornish pasties, she breathed in the smell of beef and vegetables in a flaky crust, vividly reminding her of her father's barbecues in Texas when she was a child. Going to the counter, she impulsively bought one. Taking the beef pasty out of the bag, she ate it as commuters rushed past her. Tears fell down her cheeks as she closed her eyes, savoring every bite. She could almost hear her father's voice.

Let me tell you what I know, kiddo. You're going to make it. You're stronger than you think. You're going to be fine.

It did make her feel a little better. Tossing the

bag into the trash, she looked out at Kensington High Street. The lights of the shops glimmered as car lights streaked by in the rain.

She barely remembered her mother, who'd died when she was four, but her dad had always been there. Teaching her to fish, telling her stories, helping with homework. When Emma had gotten ill as a teenager, he'd been by her side every day, even as he pulled extra overnight shifts at the factory to fight the drowning tide of medical bills.

Her throat ached. That was the kind of father her unborn baby deserved. Not a man like Cesare, who'd loved once, and lost, in a terrible tragedy, and was now unable to love anyone but himself.

Maybe it was for the best he would never know he was a father. She could just imagine how Cesare's careless lack of commitment would affect a child.

Why didn't Daddy come for my birthday, Mommy? Why doesn't he ever come see me? Doesn't he love me?

Emma's eyes narrowed. No more romantic illusions. No more false hopes. She'd never give

Cesare the chance to break their child's heart, as he'd already broken hers.

Pulling her raincoat tighter around her body, she gripped her handbag against her shoulder and went out into the drizzly night, walking down the street and past the town hall. Her footsteps echoed loudly past the expensive townhouses on Hornton Street, in counterpoint to the splatters of rain, until she finally reached Cesare's grand three-story mansion.

It was a palace of white brick, which had cost, including renovations, twenty million pounds. For years, she'd buried herself in work here, waiting for her real life to begin. Trying to decide if she even deserved a real life.

You selfish girl. Her stepmother's hoarse voice came back to her. *It should have been you who died.*

The memory still caused a spike of pain. She pushed the thought away. Marion was the one who'd ruined her father's life. She'd made a bad choice. It wasn't Emma's fault.

Though it sometimes felt that way. She swallowed. If only her father were still alive. He always had known the right thing to do....

She walked past the gate. Her lips pursed as she remembered meeting Alain Bouchard for the first time six months ago, here in the front garden. He'd shown up drunk and wanting to start a fight with Cesare, his former brother-in-law, blaming him for his sister's death. Fortunately Cesare was away, on a business trip to Berlin; Emma knew he'd never gotten over Angélique's tragic accidental death ten years before.

Emma could have called the police. That was what the rest of the staff had wanted her to do. But looking at Alain's grief-stricken face, she'd invited him into the house for tea instead, and let him talk himself out.

The next day, Alain Bouchard had sent her flowers and a handsome note of apology for his drunken ravings. That was the proper way of showing someone appreciation, Emma thought. Not by throwing expensive jewelry at them, bought in bulk, via a paid employee.

She stalked up the shadowy steps to the mansion, punched in the security code and entered. The foyer was dark, the house empty, gloomy as a tomb. None of the other staff lived in. When

Cesare was gone, which was often, she was alone. She'd spent too long in this lonely tomb.

Well, no more. Throwing down her handbag, Emma ripped off her coat and ran up the stairs, taking them two at a time. She was going to pack and leave for France immediately. Before she'd even reached her bedroom at the end of the hall, she was pulling off her knit dress, the pretty dress that hit her curves just right, that she'd bought that very day in a foolish attempt to impress Cesare. Yanking it over her head, she tossed it to the hall floor. She'd wear comfortable clothes on the train, black trousers and a plain shirt. She'd be in Paris within three hours—

A small lamp turned on by her bed. Startled, she turned.

Cesare was sitting in her antique chair with blue cushions by the marble fireplace.

She gasped, instinctively covering her lace bra and panties. "What the hell are you doing here?"

"I live here."

She straightened, and her expression hardened. "Oh, so you just remembered that, did you?"

His eyes were black in the dim light. "You

left the hotel before we could discuss something important."

"How did you—" she breathed, then cut herself off. He couldn't possibly know about the baby. And she didn't intend to let him know now.

Cesare rose to his feet, uncoiling his tall, powerful body from the chair. He looked down at her.

"I've decided not to accept your resignation," he said in a low voice. "I want you here. With me."

For a moment, they stared at each other in the shadows of her bedroom. She heard a low roll of thunder outside, the deepening patter of rain. Water dripped noisily from her hair onto the glossy hardwood floor.

Her arms dropped. She was no longer trying to cover her body. Why should she? He'd already seen everything. And she meant nothing to him. Never had. Never would.

"I don't belong here," she said. "I won't stay."

"Just because we slept together?" His eyes narrowed dangerously. "Do you really have to be such a cliché?"

"You're the cliché, not me."

"One stupid night—"

"No," she cut him off. She looked at him, and said deliberately, "I'm in love with you, Cesare."

Oh, that did it. She saw him flinch. He'd taken the words like a hit. Which was fine, because she'd meant it that way.

His black eyes glinted with fury as he grabbed her shoulders. "You don't love me. It's just because I was your first experience in bed. You haven't learned the difference between sex and love."

"But you have?"

Cesare didn't answer. He didn't have to. The whole world knew his tragic story: how he'd married young, and had been desperately in love with his wife, a beautiful French heiress, before she'd died just three years later. His heart had been buried with her.

She'd known this. And she'd still let herself hope…

Pulling away from him angrily, Emma went to her closet and reached up to the top shelf for the beat-up old suitcase that had once belonged to her father. Tossing it open on the floor, she turned back to her wardrobe to reach for her clothes.

He put his hand over hers, stilling her.

"Emma. Please."

Just that one word. The word he'd never said to her before. *Please.* She swallowed, then looked at him.

"Let me go. It's better for you this way. Better for all of us."

"I can't," he said in a low voice. "There are so few people in my life I trust. So few who actually know me. But you do. That's why I know—I *know*—you can't really love me."

His words were strangely bleak. Her heart twisted. He was right about one thing. She, of all people, did know him. She knew he was not the emotionless man the world believed him to be.

Emma ached to reach up and stroke the roughness of his cheek, to whisper words of comfort. Her hand trembled. Shadows from the closed window blinds left lines across his dark, handsome face. His eyes burned through her.

But even more: her secret burned inside her, with every beat of her heart. She was pregnant with his child. Her silence in this moment was the biggest lie any woman could tell any man.

"Why ever did you think you couldn't get pregnant, Mrs. Hayes?" her physician had asked, looking shocked. "Childhood cancer, especially ovarian cancer, can occasionally cause difficulties, yes. But in your case it worked out just fine. I see it's a surprise, but this baby is wanted, yes?"

"Of course this baby is wanted," she'd answered. Oh, yes. Emma had believed for so long that she'd never be a mother. That it wasn't even a possibility. Fighting the same deadly, silent disease years before, her mother had never been able to have another child. Caroline Hayes had ultimately died when Emma was only four, at the age of twenty-nine. Barely older than Emma was now.

"Cara." Cesare's handsome face was almost pleading as he gave an awkward laugh. "How many times did we joke about it? That I wasn't worthy of any good woman's love?"

She blinked hard. "Many times."

"So you must see. What you think you feel— it's not love. Just sex."

Hot tears burned at the backs of her eyes and she feared at any moment tears would spill over her lashes. "For *you.*"

"For both of us. You just aren't experienced

enough to realize it yet," he said gently. "But someday soon, you will..."

Emma stiffened. Was he already picturing her moving on, finding sex or love with another man? Cesare could imagine this, without it ripping out his heart?

Not Emma. It had nearly killed her to find him with Olga. And even if he hadn't slept with her—that time—she knew there had been other women. Many, many others. And there would always be.

She ripped her hand away. She didn't have to live like this. Not anymore. She'd never have to spend another lonely night staring at her ceiling, listening to the noise down the hall while he had yet another vigorous one-night stand with yet another woman he'd soon forget. She was done.

It was like a burst of sunlight and fresh air after years of imprisonment.

"I don't want to love you anymore," she whispered.

He tried to smile. "See—"

"Do you realize that I've never taken a single vacation in seven years? No personal days, no time off, except for my stepmother's funeral?"

"I just thought you were devoted to your work, like I am."

"I wasn't devoted to my work. I was devoted to *you*." She shook her head. "I've lived in London for years and still only seen Trafalgar Square from the bus. I've never been inside the museums—or even had a picture of myself taken in front of Big Ben."

He stared at her incredulously. "I'll call my driver, take you down to Trafalgar Square and take your picture myself, if that's what it takes. I'll lower your schedule to thirty hours a week and give you two months off every year." He tried to give his old charming smile. "Forget our night together, and I'll forgive your infatuation. So long as it ends now."

She shook her head. "I'm done working for you."

"And there's nothing I can do to change your mind?"

The deep, sexy timbre of his voice caused a shudder to pass through her body, all the way to her fingertips. She forced herself to ignore it.

"I can't change your nature," she choked out. "And you can't change mine. There is nothing either of us can do." She looked away. "Please ask Arthur to cut my last paycheck. I'll pick it up on the way to St. Pancras."

"St. Pancras?"

"I'm taking the train to Paris." She licked her lips. "For a new job."

He stared at her.

"You're not even giving me two weeks' notice?"

"Sorry," she mumbled.

Silence fell between them. In the distance, she heard the sounds of a police siren, with its European sound, so different from New York's.

"It seems I've been an awful boss to you these past years." Something in Cesare's tone made her look up. From where he stood on the other side of the bed, his handsome face was half-hidden in shadow. "Let me save you the trouble of a trip to the office. I'll pay you now."

"It's not necessary."

"But it is," he said coldly. In his long-sleeved black shirt and trousers, he looked sophisticated, like the international tycoon he was. But the power of his muscled shoulders and cold fury in his black eyes were anything but civilized. "Here."

Pulling a handful of fifty-pound bills out of his wallet, he tossed them toward her. Wide-eyed, Emma watched them float like feathers to the bed.

"Your paycheck," he said grimly. Reaching back into his wallet, he threw out American money next. "The vacation time you refused to take." He tossed out Euro notes. "Your Christmas bonus." Then Japanese yen. "Overtime." Dirhams and Russian rubles flew next. "The raise I should have given you."

Shocked, Emma watched the blizzard of money fall like snowflakes onto the bed, a flurry of money from all over the world, pesos and reals and kroner, dollars from Canada and Australia.

Frowning, Cesare suddenly looked into his wallet. Empty. It seemed even billionaires had a limit to ready cash. Pulling the platinum watch off his tanned wrist, he dumped it on the bed, on top of the Matterhorn of money.

"There," he said coldly. "Will that compensate you for all the anguish you suffered working for me? Are we done?"

She swallowed. Even now, in his generosity, he

was being cruel—using his wealth as a weapon against her. Making her feel small.

"Yes," she choked out. "We're done."

"So you're no longer my employee. As of this moment."

Head held high, Emma walked toward the money on the bed. *Just take it,* she told herself. She had earned that money—all of it and more! The money he'd tossed at her so carelessly was nothing to him, barely more than he might spend impulsively on an amusing night out, buying thousand-pound bottles of scotch for all his rich friends.

But still. There was something truly awful about reaching for a pile of money left on her bed. Something sordid.

She tried to force herself forward, then stiffened. She exhaled, pulling back her hand.

"What's wrong now?"

"I can't take it," she said. "Not like this."

He slowly walked around the bed toward her. "It's yours. You earned it."

"Earned it how?" she whispered.

"For God's sake, Emma!"

She whirled back to him. "I can't take it off the *bed*. As if I were your..."

She couldn't say the word, but he did.

"My whore?" Cesare came toward her, his dark eyes like fire. "You are driving me insane," he ground out. "If you do not want the money, then leave it. If you are so determined to go, then go. I don't give a damn what you do."

"You've made that painfully clear," she said hoarsely.

"And you," he snarled, "have made it clear that there is no way I can win. You think I'm a selfish bastard, you hate me, you hate yourself for your so-called *love* for me. You're sick of the sight of me and you're using our night together as an excuse to quit."

She sucked in her breath.

"An *excuse?*" It was humiliating how her voice squeaked on the word.

"Yes." Cesare was close to her now, very close. She was suddenly very aware that she was wearing almost nothing and they were alone in her dark bedroom. Her nipples were hard beneath her white lace bra. Her own breathing seemed loud in her ears. His powerful body towered over hers, and she could feel the warmth emanating off his skin. The heat in his gaze scared her—almost as much as the answering heat in her own body. He said in a low voice, "You're running away from me like a coward."

She gasped, "Are you kidding? *I'm* running like a coward?"

Cesare's hand reached out to touch her cheek, and as she felt his fingertips against her skin, it was all she could do not to turn her face into the warmth of his caress, even now. "You mean nothing to me, Emma," he growled. His dark eyes burned through her. "You never have. You never will."

"Good," she choked out. "Because I can hardly wait to leave you. I'm so happy that after tonight I'll never see you again…."

His hand trailed down her cheek, to her neck, to her bare shoulder. She barely heard his harsh intake of breath over the pounding of her own heart. She trembled, knowing she was on the knife's edge.

Cesare roughly seized her in his arms, and crushed her lips with his own.

CHAPTER THREE

CESARE'S KISS WAS angry and searing. His lips plundered hers, and all her anger and grief and pain seemed to explode beneath the fire of his touch, into an inferno.

He wrapped a strong arm around her waist, holding her tight against him, and his other hand ran along her bare arm, up her shoulder, down her naked back. She felt his body, hard against hers, and against her will a soft moan came from the back of her throat. Her skin felt scorched everywhere he touched. She was desperate to have him closer.

Now.

Her hand cupped the rough edge of his jawline, then moved back to tangle in his dark hair, pulling his mouth harder and deeper into hers.

She heard his hoarse intake of breath as he cupped her full, aching breasts over the lace of her bra. She was overflowing the cups now, and her belly was starting to get fuller as well. Would he notice? Would he guess? Would Cesare be able to see how he'd permanently branded her body as his, always and forever, without her saying a single word?

"All this time, I've been hating myself for a lack of self-control," he said in a low voice. "Now I can hardly believe I had such restraint." He lifted his gaze to hers, even as one of his hands slowly stroked her nearly naked body, over her white lace, causing her to tremble with need. "I can't believe I waited so long." His sensual lips curved as he cupped her face, tilting back her head. "No other woman has even interested me since that night...."

Her lips parted. No. Surely he couldn't mean what she thought he meant....

With their bodies so close, standing together beside her bed, she felt his warmth and strength. She breathed in the bare hint of masculine cologne. She felt the electricity of his words, of his touch—the overwhelming sensual force of his complete attention. And Emma's only defense, anger, crumbled.

He kissed her softly, briefly, butterfly kisses

to each of her cheeks, tantalizingly close to the corners of her mouth. But hope, like a fragile spring bud unfolding in the snow, began to build inside her. She could hardly believe his shocking confession.

He'd been faithful....

"There's really been no other woman for you since our night?" she breathed.

He shook his head, his eyes dark. "Has there been someone for you?"

The question made her choke out a laugh. "How could there be?"

"Does that mean no?"

"Of course not!"

"Good."

His sudden masculine smugness irritated her. "You admit something, too," she said sharply.

"What?"

"You didn't seduce me three months ago just because I was crying. You weren't just trying to comfort me."

He stared at her, then said quietly, "No."

Her soul thrilled at the concession. She gloried in it. "You wanted me, too."

He spoke a single grudging word, as if it were pulled from deep inside him. "Yes."

"For how long?"

"Years," he bit out.

"Why didn't you tell me?" she whispered.

"I was afraid you'd do exactly what you did today." His hands undid the plaits of her braids, causing her long dark hair to fall down her back. She trembled as his hands stroked her long, tumbling waves of hair. "You'd get some crazy delusion of loving me, and then I'd have to fire you."

"I am in love with you."

He snorted. "If you really loved me, wouldn't you be begging me to stay?"

"Because begging works so well with you."

Slowly he lowered his head until his mouth was inches from hers.

"It's just lust, *cara*," he whispered, his lips almost brushing hers. "Not love…."

And holding her against his hard body in the shadowy bedroom, he kissed her, clutching her as if he were a drowning man and only she could save him. His lips plundered hers, teasing, gentling, searing.

As they stood together, he slowly kissed down

her throat, his fingertips roaming softly over her naked skin. She felt the warmth of his hands cupping her breasts, stroking tight, aching nipples that peeked through white lace.

Leaning back in his arms, she gasped with pleasure and need. Until she lost her balance, and fell back against the bed, his arms still around her, their bodies entangled in their embrace.

The bed felt made of feathers beneath her. Still in her bra and panties, Emma slid against the duvet cover, and felt something sharp and cold beneath her thigh. She pulled it out and looked at the shining platinum face with confusion. "Your watch."

"Forget it." Taking it from her hand, he tossed the expensive watch across the room, causing it to scatter noisily across the hardwood floor before it hit the wall with a soft thunk.

She realized what the "feathers" she'd felt beneath her body actually had to be. Twisting, she tried to look beneath her. She was lying almost naked beneath him *on a bed of money.* "Everything's still on the bed—"

"I don't care," he said roughly, and kissed her,

until she forgot about the money, and wouldn't have cared if she did.

Pulling away, he pulled off his shirt in an abrupt movement. Emma's throat constricted as she reached out to touch the intoxicating vision of his naked chest, muscular and hard, with tanned skin that felt like silk over steel. She stroked down to the flat six-pack of his belly, laced with a scattering of dark hair. He was flesh and blood, this man she'd wanted so hopelessly, and loved for so long.

Covering her body with his own, Cesare kissed her. She felt his weight crushing her breasts, felt the slide of his warm bare skin against her own. He released the clasp of her bra and pulled off the slip of white lace, tossing it aside. He pulled her panties slowly past her hips, over her thighs, down her legs.

She was naked beneath him. Lying on a pile of money. She shouldn't be doing this, she thought. Then he pulled off his pants and silk boxers, and rational thought left her entirely.

She gasped as she saw how large he was, how huge and hard. Slowly, he kissed down her body, licking and suckling her breasts. He caressed down the curve of her belly, then kissed her lips in a long, deep embrace that seemed to last forever, until she forgot where she ended and he began. Their bodies fused together in heat, skin to skin, slick and salty and sweet. Moving down her body, he pushed her legs apart with his knee, spreading them wide with his hands. Lowering his head, he nuzzled between her thighs. She felt his hot breath.

She gasped as, holding her hips firmly against the bed, he spread her wide and tasted her.

She twisted, rocking beneath him. The pleasure was too sharp, too explosive. Beneath the ruthless insistence of his tongue, she trembled and shook, gasping on the bed. Every time she moved, money went flying into the air. Durhams and dollars, pounds and pesos flew violently, then fell back softly like snow, sliding down the naked bodies clutched together on the bed.

The money felt whisper-soft, brushing against Emma's face or shoulder or breast while she felt the hard, bristly roughness of his masculine body between her legs.

"Lust," Cesare said in a low voice.

Their eyes locked over the curves of her naked body. She shook her head.

"Love…"

With a low growl, he lowered his head back between her legs. She felt the heat of his breath on her tender skin, and his tongue took another wide taste of her, then another. Slowly he caressed her, licking her in delicate swirls until her breathing came in gasps and her hands were gripping the bedsheets beneath her, along with fistfuls of yen and euros.

"Lust," he whispered against her skin.

"No," she choked out.

He thrust his tongue an inch inside her. She gave a shocked gasp in a voice she hardly recognized as her own. His hands roamed possessively over her, cupping her breasts, her waist, her hips. Reaching beneath her, he pressed her bottom upward, lifting her more firmly against his mouth, and impaled her more deeply with his tongue. His lips and soft wet tongue suckled the aching center of her need as he moved two thick fingertips inside her, where his tongue had been. She cried out, overwhelmed by the intensity of pleasure.

Her back arched from the feel of his fingers inside her and his tongue swirling over her and she gripped his shoulders as waves of ecstasy started to pull reality beneath her feet, crashing over her. She exploded, and as if from a distance, she heard herself scream—

Rolling beside her, he pulled her into the warm haven of his arms. Emma looked up at him with tears in her eyes.

It wasn't just lust between them. It *wasn't.*

If he'd only just give her a chance. If only he'd say something that would make her think she could tell him about the baby…

Leaning up, Emma put her hand on his cheek and kissed him in a deep, lingering embrace that left her chin and cheeks tingling from the rough bristles of his jaw. She could still feel his body straining against her. As he kissed her back, holding her tight, breathless hope ripped through her. She could show him he had nothing to fear. That their relationship could be so much more than lust. She knew the man he really was, yes. But she also knew the man he could be.…

"Love," she whispered silently against his lips.

Emma abruptly rolled him beneath her on the

bed. He looked up at her, surprised. She smiled, her soul welling up with sudden certain joy. If he wouldn't let her speak words of love…

She would show him.

Cesare stared up at the woman who'd just rolled him beneath her on the bed. He felt Emma's hands stroke down his chest, as her legs straddled his hips.

She was so impossibly beautiful, he thought, dazzled by the pink flush of her creamy skin, the emerald gleam of her eyes. She looked down at him fiercely, like an ancient warrior queen who commanded an army of thousands eager to die in her name. Power emanated from her proud, curvaceous body like light. Power he'd never seen in her before.

"Emma," he breathed. "What's gotten into you?"

"Haven't you figured it out?" Her full red lips curved into a smile as she lowered her head. She whispered against his mouth, "You have."

She kissed him, and he felt that something had changed in her. Something he didn't understand. She seemed—different. New. Beneath her touch, sparks flew up and down his body, a fire that burned him to blood and bone.

He'd wanted her for months. Years. But never like this. His body shook with need. She'd never, ever made the first move before.

He could hardly believe he'd once thought of Emma as having no feelings. This was who she really was: a seductive sex goddess, innocent and wanton, powerful and glorious...

As her lips caressed his, her long dark hair tumbled over his body, sliding over his overheated skin. Her full breasts brushed against his chest. With a moan, he cupped them with his hands. Breaking off their kiss, he wrenched his head to suckle a taut, pink nipple, licking it, pulling it into his mouth. His hand tangled in her hair, stroking down her naked back. He heard her moan. Felt her thighs tighten around his hips. He felt the soft, wet core of her brush the tip of his hardest edge as she swayed in innocently tantalizing torture.

Twisting away with a choked gasp, he started to reach for the wallet in his jacket hanging on a nearby chair, intending to retrieve a condom, but she stopped him.

"It's not necessary." She hesitated, then said slowly, "This time because I'm actually—"

"You're still on the Pill?" He exhaled. "Thank God." She stiffened, and he wondered if he'd said something rude, though he couldn't imagine what. Women could be sensitive, and even though Emma was the most rational woman he knew, she was still undeniably a woman. Oh, yes. Running his hand down the curve of her bare breast—even fuller than he remembered—he looked up at her with heavy-lidded eyes. "I love that you are always prepared, Miss Hayes."

She leaned forward, allowing her long dark hair to trail sensuously across his bare chest as she said pointedly, "Emma."

"Emma," he groaned as her fingertips trailed down his body. "Oh, God—Emma—"

Reaching up, he kissed her, and as she leaned down to kiss him back, he could wait no longer. Pulling her down on him with his hands, he simultaneously thrust up with his hips, pushing inside her, and heard her gasp as he filled her soft, wet body.

God. He'd never felt anything like this. He rammed inside her, filling her hard and deep. She slid over his hips, riding him, and his whole body started to tighten. No. No, it was too soon. The intensity of pleasure was too much. But being inside her without a condom…skin to skin…

He gripped her shoulders. "I'm not sure how long I can last," he said hoarsely. "Give me… Give me a minute to…"

But it seemed Emma's days of obedience were over. She continued to slide against him. He looked up, intending to protest. He stopped when he saw how her eyes were closed, her beautiful face rapt and shining in ecstasy.

No! He squeezed his eyes shut. He couldn't see her like that! Not when at any moment he could… He could… But even with his eyes closed, he could still see her shining face, see her full breasts swaying above him as she moved. He felt tighter—tighter—about to explode…

"You feel so good," she whispered. "So—good…"

"Oh, my God," he said in a strangled voice. "Stop!"

Gripping his shoulders, she leaned forward, so close he could feel the brush of her lips against his earlobe, and whispered, "Love."

It was the one thing that made him cold.

"Lust," he growled back, and flung his body over hers, lying her beneath him on the bed. He ran his hands down her body, licking and sucking every inch of her skin. Sitting back against the pillows, he pulled her into his lap, wrapping his arms around her.

Tangling his hands in her hair, he tilted back her head and kissed her deeply. Lifting up her body, he lowered her hips heavily against him, thrusting slowly inside her. He rocked against her, controlling the rhythm and speed, slowing down when he came too close to exploding. Face-to-face, breath to breath, their eyes locked, their arms wrapped around each other, as close as two lovers could possibly be. He made love to her for what felt like hours until finally she gasped against him one more time, closing her eyes with a cry.

Cesare could hold back no longer. Kissing her shoulder, he sucked hard against her skin, and let himself go. He thrust inside her four times, so deep and hard that he exploded, so close to heaven that he saw only stars.

He saw only *her.*

Exhaling, he collapsed, still holding her tight.

It took long moments for Cesare to fall back to earth. He slowly became aware of the ticking of the old antique clock on the mantel. Blinking in the darkness, he saw he was in Emma's bed, in her suite of rooms on the second floor of his Kensington house. Moonlight was creeping in through the edges of the window shades as he still cradled her in his arms. He felt her cheek against his chest. Against his heart.

He shifted, cuddling her in the crook of his arm, her naked body against his own. He saw a small mark on her shoulder, where he'd sucked a little too hard in a love bite. That would leave a bruise, he thought. He'd marked her as his own. And for some reason he didn't want to examine, he was glad.

Emma blinked, smiling up at him sleepily before she glanced down at the bed. "What a mess we've made."

He looked down. The duvet and sheets were twisted at their feet and there were banknotes *everywhere.*

Cesare prided himself on discipline. He'd tried to do the sensible thing with Emma, to make them both forget their intoxicating night and return to their employer-employee relationship.

He'd failed. Massively.

And he was glad.

Now they could both have what they actually wanted. Yes, his home might fall apart without her in charge. At the moment he didn't give a damn. Who cared about milk in the fridge or having his bed made perfectly? Who cared about it being made at all, so long as he had her in it?

Emma yawned, her eyes closing as she settled deeper into his arms. Leaning forward, he kissed her softly on the temple. His own eyelids were heavy.

As she drowsed in his arms, he still shuddered with aftershocks of pleasure from their lovemaking. Making love without a condom, to a woman he liked and trusted, was a wholly new experience.

He'd certainly never had it with his wife.

Cesare looked down at Emma's face, half-hidden in shadow as she slept in his arms. She looked like a slumbering angel, her black eyelashes stark against her pale skin, and masses of her long, glossy dark hair tumbling over the pillow.

He felt exhausted, utterly spent. But as he closed his eyes, he smiled. He'd proved his point, and he was suddenly glad Emma had quit her job with him. That meant she'd be available for full-time pleasure. Their relationship might last for weeks, even months, now she understood there was no love involved. There would be no arguments, no goals of marriage or children to fight over. They could just enjoy each other's company for as long as the pleasure lasted.... He fell asleep, smiling and warm.

When he woke, the shadows of the room had changed to the soft gray light of dawn. Emma was stirring in his arms. He saw she was looking up at him with big, limpid eyes.

"Good morning," she said shyly.

Cesare stroked her cheek with amusement. "Good morning."

She bit her lip. "Um. If you want to go sleep in your own room, I'll understand...."

He placed a finger to her lips, gently stopping her. "I don't."

Her expression suddenly glowed. "You don't?"

He didn't blame her for being surprised. He was somewhat surprised himself. Usually he couldn't wait to get out of a woman's bed the morning after. He usually left long before morning, in fact.

But he felt oddly comfortable with Emma. He didn't need to pretend with her, or play games, or be polite. It was strange, but he felt like he could just be himself, without trying to hide his flaws. How could he hide them? She knew them all.

"I'm hungry," Emma confessed, sitting up. "I can't stop thinking about fried eggs and bacon and oranges…"

Cesare kissed her bare shoulder. He was not thinking about food. "We could go down to the kitchen." He let his fingertips trail over her breast. "Or we could have a little breakfast in bed first…."

"Yes," she whispered, lifting her lips toward his. He stroked back her wildly tousled black hair.

"I'm so glad you came to your senses," he murmured as he kissed her.

She drew back with a frown. "My senses?"

He smiled, twisting a long black tendril of her hair around his finger. "You are going to be a very enjoyable bit of carry-on baggage."

"Oh, so now I'm baggage, am I?"

"I've decided you were right."

Her green eyes suddenly shone. "You did?"

"I'm glad you quit," he said lazily, running the pad of his thumb over her nipple, for the masculine pleasure of watching it instantly pebble beneath his touch. "I need to be in Asia tomorrow, Berlin on Friday."

Lifting a dark eyebrow, she said lightly, "And I need to take that job in Paris."

"You're thinking about your job?" He snorted. "I want you to come with me."

"Give up my career to do what—just hang out in your bed?"

"Can you think of a better idea?"

"I like my career." Her voice had a new edge to it. "I'm good at it."

"Of course you are. The best," he said soothingly. He hadn't meant to insult her. "But I'll cover your expenses while you're with me. We can just both enjoy ourselves. For however long this lasts."

"Are you joking?" She sounded almost angry.

Cesare was still waiting for her burst of excited joy and arms to be thrown around him at the brilliance of his plan. Her joy didn't seem to be forthcoming. "Don't you understand what I'm offering you, Emma?"

"I must not," she said. "Because it sounds like you expect me to drop everything for you, when all you want is sex."

"Sex with *you*," he pointed out. He would have thought that would be obvious. "And friendship," he added as an afterthought. "It'll be…fun."

"Fun?" she said in a strangled voice.

"What's wrong with that?"

"Nothing. Wow. It's the answer to all my childhood dreams. *Fun*."

He was starting to grow irritated "You can throw away your mop and broom. No more twenty-four-hour days with a jerk for a boss." He tried to laugh, but she didn't join him at the joke. He continued weakly, "You'll travel with me—see the world…"

Pulling away from him entirely, she looked at him in the gray dawn.

"For how long?" she said quietly.

"How should I know?" Sitting up straighter against the headboard, he folded his arms grumpily. "For as long as we're enjoying ourselves."

"And you'll kindly pay me for my time."

He ground his jaw. "You're twisting this all around, making it sound like I'm trying to insult you. Why aren't you happy? You should be happy—I've never offered any woman so much!"

She rebelliously lifted her eyes. "We both know that's not true."

A cold chill went down his spine. "You're talking about my wife."

She didn't answer. She didn't have to.

"Christo." Cesare clawed back his hair. This couldn't be happening. "We've been together only two nights, I've barely asked you to be my mistress, and you're already pressuring me to marry you?"

"I didn't say that!"

"You don't have to." He could see it in her face: that terrible repressed hope. The same expression he'd seen in so many women's faces. The desire to pin him down, to hold him against his will, in a place he didn't want to be. To make iron chains of duty and honor replace delight or even pleasure.

"You did get married once. You must have had a reason."

Anger rushed through him. The memory of

Alain Bouchard's hateful voice. *You married my sister for her money and then made her life a living hell. Is it any wonder she took the pills? You might as well have poured them down her throat.*

Cesare's lips parted to lash out. Then he forced himself to focus on Emma's lovely, wistful face. It wasn't her fault. He choked back furious, hateful words.

"I married for love once," he said flatly. "I'll never do it again."

"Because you still love her," she whispered. "Your wife."

Cesare could see what Emma believed. That he'd loved Angélique so much that even a decade hadn't been enough to get over the grief of losing her. He let it pass, as he always did. The beautiful, simple lie was so much better than the truth.

He set his jaw, facing her across the bed, not touching. Just moments before, they'd been so close. Now an ocean divided them.

"I thought I made myself clear. But it wasn't enough. So hear this." He looked at her. "I will never love you, Emma. I will never marry you. I will never want to have a child with you. Ever."

In the rising pink dawn, every ounce of color

drained from Emma's beautiful, plump-cheeked face, causing the powerful light of joy to disappear, as if it had never existed.

It was hard to watch. Cesare took a steadying breath. He had to be cruel to be kind. If they were to be together, even for just a few weeks, she had to accept these things from the beginning.

"My feelings in this matter will never change," he said quietly. "I thought you understood. I thought you felt the same." He reached for her hand, trembling where it rested on the bed. "Lust."

In a flash of anguish, her luminous eyes lifted to his. She shook her head. His eyes narrowed.

"You must accept this," he said, "for us to have any future."

A low, bitter laugh bubbled to her lips—the most bitter thing he'd ever heard from her. She ripped her hand away. "Future? No love, no marriage, no child. What kind of future is that?"

His jaw tightened. "The kind that is real. No promises to be broken. No pretense. No fakery. We just take it day by day, enjoying each other's company, taking pleasure for as long as it lasts."

"And then what?"

"We part as friends." He looked at her. "I don't want to lose your friendship."

"My friendship?" Her lip curled. "Or my services?"

"Emma!"

"You want to stop paying me as your housekeeper, and hire me straight out as your whore. No, I get it." Holding up her hand, she said coldly, "I'm sorry, this is awkward for you, isn't it? Usually I'm the one who handles this, who puts out your trash the morning after." She looked past the tangled mess of bedcovers at the foot of the bed, still surrounded by an explosion of money, to his platinum watch lying on the floor. "You even gave me a watch. Just like all the rest."

His own personal watch was even more expensive than the Cartier ones, but he sensed telling her that wouldn't impress her. "Emma, you're being idiotic...."

"I really am just like the rest." She threw the sheets aside and stood up from the bed. "I'll just collect my things and buy myself some roses on the high street, shall I?"

But as she started to walk away from the bed, Cesare grabbed her wrist.

"Don't do this," he said in a low voice.

"Do what?"

"This." He looked up at her, his eyes glittering. "I want you in my bed. For now. For as long as it's fun for both of us. Can't that be enough? Why do you need false promises of more? Why can't you just accept what I freely offer you?"

Their eyes locked. He could see the pain in her gaze.

"I want more. I want it all," she whispered. "Love. Marriage." She swallowed, looking up at him. "I want a baby. Our baby."

The air around him suddenly felt thin. He shrank back from her words. Literally. "Emma…"

"I don't need a wedding proposal. Or for you to say you're ready to be a father." Her eyes met his. "I just need to know you might want those things someday." She blinked fast. "That you might be open to the possibility…if something ever…"

"No," Cesare choked out. Still naked, he scrambled back on the bed, putting his hand to his neck, feeling as if he had something tight around his throat. He took a deep breath, forcing his hands down, trying to calm down, to breathe.

"Either this is a fun diversion, a friendship with benefits, or it's nothing. You decide."

She stared at him for a long moment, her face as pale as marble. Then, violently, she grabbed her white bra and panties off the floor and yanked them on her body. Walking to her closet, she pulled out big armfuls of clothes. "What was I thinking—" she kicked open her old suitcase "—to believe—" she tossed the clothes inside "—in miracles!"

Cesare rose to his feet. Still naked, he padded across the hardwood floor. Without her warmth next to him, the bedroom felt chilly in the autumn morning. He heard traffic noise from the street outside. Soon, the house's day staff would arrive. He desperately wanted this settled before they were interrupted. He felt Emma was slipping away from him. He didn't understand why. With a deep breath, he tried once more.

"Why are you throwing everything away for the sake of some distant future? Think about today." Wrapping his arms around her waist from behind, he nuzzled the side of her neck and said in a low voice, "Let tomorrow take care of itself…."

Her skin was cold to the touch. She pulled away. Her beautiful face looked more than forlorn now—she looked frozen.

He sucked in his breath. He searched her face. "You're still going to leave, aren't you," he breathed. "You're still going to throw everything away for dreams of love, marriage and children. For a *delusion*. I can't believe you'd be such a…"

Emma's eyes were stony. She looked as if her soul had been shattered.

"…fool?" she finished.

He gave a single stiff nod.

She shook her head, wiping her eyes. "You're right. I have been a fool. A stupid romantic fool who believed a man like you could ever change."

Kneeling down, she gathered all the piles of money off the floor and dumped it into her suitcase. Picking up the platinum watch, she tossed it inside, then closed the suitcase with a bang. She looked down.

"Thank you for your offer," she said in a low voice. "I'm sure some other woman will take you up on it." She looked up, her eyes luminous with tears. "But I'm going to have a baby, and a home. And a man who loves us both."

Her words, spoken with such finality, hit him like a blow. He'd just offered Emma more than he'd offered any woman in ten years. And this was his reward for letting himself be vulnerable. Though he stood in front of Emma right now in flesh and blood, she was still rejecting him for some ridiculous fantasy of love and a child.

Something Cesare hadn't felt in a long, long time—something he'd thought he would never feel again—sliced through his heart.

Hurt.

His arms dropped. He stepped back.

"Bene," he said stiffly. "Go."

She pulled on jeans and a T-shirt. She picked up a few errant fifty-dollar banknotes off the floor and tucked them securely in her pocket, then lifted her chin. "Don't worry. I won't bother you again. I'll leave you alone to live the life you want. I give you my word." She held out her hand as if they were strangers. "Goodbye, Cesare."

His lips tightened, but he shook her hand.

"Arrivederci, Signorina Hayes. I hope you find what you're looking for."

Her green eyes shimmered, and she turned away without a word. Gathering her suitcase, her coat and her bag, Emma left the tidy bedroom. Cesare listened to her suitcase *thump, thump, thump* down his stairs. He listened to the front door open—and then latch closed.

She'd really gone. He couldn't believe it.

Going to the window, he looked down and watched her walk away, down the sidewalk toward Kensington High Street, in the drizzling rain of London's gray morning. He watched her small, forlorn figure with an old suitcase and a beige mackintosh, and felt a strange twist in his chest.

It's better this way, he told himself fiercely. Better for her to go, before the small hole in his heart had a chance to grow any larger. He watched her get smaller and smaller.

"Go," Cesare said aloud in the empty room. "You mean nothing to me."

But still, his hands tightened at his sides. *She'll be back,* he thought suddenly. No woman he wanted had ever been able to resist for long. And the sex had been too good between them. Emma wouldn't be able to stay away.

She'd soon be back, begging to negotiate the terms of her surrender. He exhaled, his shoulders relaxing. He allowed himself a smile. She'd be back. He knew it.

Within the week, if not the day.

CHAPTER FOUR

Ten months later

CESARE LOOKED OUT the window as his driver pulled the Rolls-Royce smoothly through the traffic of the Quai Branly, past the Pont de l'Alma. The September sun was sparkling like diamonds on the Seine.

Paris was not Cesare's favorite city. Yes, the city was justly famous for its beauty, but it was also aloof and proud. Like a coquette. Like a cold, distant star. Like his late wife, Angélique, who was born here—and took her lover here, a scant year after their marriage.

Sì. He had reason to dislike Paris. Since his wife's death over a decade before, he'd avoided the city. But now he was building a Falconeri Hotel here, upon the demand of his shareholders.

But Paris had changed since his last visit, he realized. The city felt…different.

Cesare looked up at the elegant classical architecture of cream-colored buildings. Through the vivid yellows and reds of the trees, the golden sun was bright in the blue sky. The city had a new warmth and charm he'd never felt before.

Because we finished the business deal, he told himself. After months of mind-numbing negotiations, his team had finally completed the purchase of an old, family-run hotel on the Avenue Montaigne, which—after it was exhaustively remodeled—would become the first Falconeri Hotel in France. *I'm just pleased about the deal.*

But he shifted in his leather seat. Even he didn't buy that.

Closing his eyes, he felt the sun on his skin. Against his will, he thought of her, and his body flashed with heat that had nothing to do with sunlight.

Emma lived in Paris.

You don't know that, he told himself fiercely. It had been almost a year since she'd left him in London that dreary November morning. For all he knew, she'd moved on to another job, another city. For all he knew, she'd changed her mind and never taken a job in Paris at all. For all he knew, she'd found another lover, a man who would love and marry her and be willing to have a child with her, just as she'd wanted.

For all he knew, she was already his wife. Pregnant with his child.

Cesare's hands tightened involuntarily.

For ten months, he'd made a point of not knowing where Emma was or whom she was with. He'd told himself he didn't care. At first, he'd been sure she'd soon return. It had taken him months to finally accept she wasn't coming back. Cesare knew she'd wanted him, as he wanted her. He'd been surprised to discover she'd wanted her dreams even more.

He'd been furious, hurt; and yet he'd respected her the more for it. She was the one who'd gotten away. The one he couldn't have. But she'd made the right choice. They wanted different things in life. Emma wanted a love, a home, a husband and a family of her own.

Cesare wanted—

What was it he wanted?

He tapped his fingers on the leather armrest as he stared out at the sparkling river. More, he supposed. More money. More hotels. More success for his company. More, more, more of the same, same, same.

His PR firm would soon announce how absolutely ecstatic the Falconeri Group was to finally have a hotel in this spectacular French city. His lips twisted. Well, Cesare would be ecstatic to leave it. This magical city seemed to have a strange power to steal any woman he actually tried to keep for longer than a night.

He wondered suddenly if Emma's dreams had been haunted, as his had been. Or if all she felt for him now was indifference. If she'd forgotten him entirely. If he alone was cursed with the inability to forget.

His driver stopped at a red light. Resentfully Cesare watched smiling tourists cross the street, walking from the popular *bateaux* of the Seine to the nearby Eiffel Tower. He still saw Emma in his dreams at night. Still felt her breath against his skin. Still heard her voice. Even by the light of day—hell, even now—his feverish imagination...

Cesare's eyes widened as he saw a woman crossing the street. She passed by quickly, before he could see her face. But he saw the black, glossy hair tumbling down her shoulders, saw the way her hips swayed and the luscious curve of her petite frame as she walked away from him. No. It couldn't be her. This woman was pushing a baby stroller. No, he was imagining things. Paris was a city of over two million people. There was no way that...

Cesare gripped the headrest of the seat in front of him.

"Stop the car," he said softly.

The chauffeur frowned, looking at Cesare in the rearview mirror. "Monsieur?" he said, sounding puzzled. When the light turned green, he drove the Rolls-Royce forward with traffic.

Cesare watched the woman continue walking away. It couldn't be Emma for a million reasons, the most obvious being the stroller.

Unless she'd really meant what she said about finding a man who would give her a child, and she'd done it in a hurry.

I'm going to have a baby. And a home. And a man who loves us both.

Watching her disappear down the street, he remembered the cold, gray morning last November, when he'd watched Emma walk down Hornton

Street. He'd been so sure she'd come back. She never had. Not a message. Not a word.

He watched this woman go, with one last sway of her hips, one last shimmering beam of sunlight on her long, glossy black hair, before she turned toward the Champ de Mars. Disappearing...again...

Cesare twisted his head savagely toward the driver. "Damn you!" he exploded. "I said stop!"

Looking a little frightened, the driver immediately plunged through traffic to the side of the road. The Rolls-Royce hadn't even completely stopped before Cesare opened the door and flung himself on the sidewalk, causing several pedestrians to scatter. People stared at Cesare like he was crazy.

He felt crazy. He turned his head right and left as he started to run, getting honked at angrily by a tour bus as he crossed the street.

Where was the dark-haired woman? Had he lost her? Had it been Emma? He clawed his dark hair back, looking around frantically.

"Attention—monsieur!"

He moved just in time to avoid getting run over by a baby carriage pushed by a gray-haired woman dressed in Gucci. *"Excusez-moi, madame,"* he murmured. She shook her head in irritation, huffing. Even Parisian grandmothers, even the *nannies,* wore designer clothes in this arrondissement.

He ran down the Avenue de la Bourdonnais, where he'd last seen her, and followed the crowds into the nearby park, the Champ de Mars, looking right and left, turning himself in circles. He walked beneath the shadow of the Eiffel Tower, past long queues of people. He walked down the paths of the park, past cheery couples and families having picnic lunches on this beautiful autumn day. Wearing his suit and tie, Cesare felt unbearably hot, running all over Paris in pursuit of a phantom from his past.

Cesare stopped.

He heard the soft whir of the wind through the trees, and looked up at the blue sky, through leaves that were a million different shades of green, yellow, orange. He heard the crunch of gravel beneath his feet. He heard children's laughter and music. In the distance, he saw a small outdoor snack stand, and beyond that, a playground with a merry-go-round.

What the hell was he doing?

Cesare clawed back his hair. *Basta.* Enough. Scowling, he walked to the snack stand and bought himself a coffee, then did something no true Parisian would ever do in a million years— he drank it as he walked. The black, scalding-hot coffee burned his tongue. He drank it all down, then tossed the empty cup in the trash. Grimly he reached into his pocket for his cell phone, to call his driver and get back on schedule, back to sanity, and return to the private airport on the east of the city where his jet waited. Walking, he lifted the cell phone to his ear. "Olivier, you can come get me at…"

He heard a woman gasp.

"Cesare?"

He froze.

Emma's voice. Her sweet voice.

"Sir?" his driver said at the other end of the line.

But Cesare's arm had already gone limp, the phone dropping to his side. Even now, he was telling himself that it wasn't her, it couldn't possibly be.

He turned.

"Emma," he whispered.

She was standing in front of a park bench, the stroller beside her. Her green eyes were wide and it seemed to Cesare in this moment like every bit of sunlight had fled the sky to caress her pink blouse, her brown slacks, her long black hair with a halo of brilliant golden light. The rest of the park faded from sight. There was only *her,* shining like a star, ripping through his cold soul like fire.

"It is you," she breathed. She blinked, looking back uneasily at the stroller before she turned back, biting her lip. "What are you…doing here?"

"I'm here…" His voice was rough. He cleared his throat. "On business."

"But you hate this city. I've heard you say so."

"I bought an old hotel on the Avenue Montaigne. Just this morning."

He'd somehow walked all the way to her without realizing it. His eyes drank her in hungrily. Her cheeks were fuller, her pale skin pink as roses. Her dark hair fell in tumbling soft waves over her shoulders. She'd put on a little weight, he saw, and it suited her well. The womanly softness made her even more beautiful, something he wouldn't have thought possible.

"It's—a surprise to see you," she faltered.

"Yes." His eyes fell on a dark-haired, fat-cheeked baby sleeping in the stroller. Who was this baby? Perhaps the child of her employer? Or could it possibly be…hers? His gaze quickly fell to her left hand. No wedding ring.

So the baby couldn't be hers, then. She'd been very specific about what she'd said she wanted. *A husband, a home, a baby.* She surely wouldn't have settled for less—not after she'd left him for the sake of those dreams.

The pink in Emma's cheeks deepened. "You didn't come searching for me?"

His pride wanted him to say it was pure coincidence he'd stumbled upon her in the park. But he couldn't.

"I came to Paris for the deal," he said quietly. "But on my way out of town, I thought I saw you cross the street. And I couldn't leave without knowing if it was you."

They stood facing each other in the sunlit park, just inches away, not touching. He dimly heard birds sing in the trees above, the distant traffic of tour buses at the Eiffel Tower, the laughter of children at the merry-go-round.

"I was so sure you would return to me," he heard himself say in a low voice. "But you never did."

Her green eyes scorched through his heart. Then, in a voice almost too quiet to hear, she said, "I...couldn't."

"I know." Before he even realized what he was doing, he'd reached out a hand to her cheek.

Her skin was even softer than he remembered. He felt her shiver beneath his touch, and his body ignited. He wanted to take her in his arms, against his body, to kiss her hard and never let go.

Just moments before, he'd felt admiration about how she'd sacrificed the pleasure they might have had together, in order to pursue her true dreams. But in this instant, all those rational considerations were swept aside. He searched her gaze. "Did you ever wonder what we could have had?"

A shadow crossed her face.

"Of course I did."

He barely heard the noises around them, the soft coo of the baby, the chatter around them in a multitude of languages as tourists strolled by.

He'd missed her.

Not just her housekeeping skills. Nor even her sensual body.

Emma Hayes was the only woman he'd ever trusted. The only one he'd ever let himself care about, since the nightmare of his marriage so long ago.

Standing with Emma in this park in the center of Paris, Cesare would have given a million euros to see her smile at him the way she used to. To hear her voice gently mocking him, teasing him, putting him politely but firmly in his place. They'd had their own private language, he saw that now, and he suddenly realized how unusual that was. How special and rare.

No one called him on his arrogance anymore. No one else could challenge him with a single dimpled smile. No one kept him on his toes. Kept him breathless with longing.

He'd found a different housekeeper to keep his kitchen stocked and do his laundry. Perhaps, someday, he'd find a woman equally alluring to fill his bed. But who could fill the void that Emma had left in his life?

She'd been more than his housekeeper. More than his lover. She'd been his friend.

His hand moved down her neck to her shoulder. He felt her warmth through the soft pink fabric of her blouse.

"Come back to London with me," he said suddenly.

She blinked, then, glancing at her baby, she licked her lips. Her voice seemed hoarse as she asked, "Why?"

Cesare hesitated. If there was one thing he'd learned in life, it was that a man should never show weakness. Not even with a woman. *Especially* not with a woman. "The housekeeper I hired to replace you has been unsatisfactory."

"Oh." With a sigh, she looked down. "Sorry. I am working for someone else now. He's been good to me. I have no desire to leave him."

I have no desire to leave him. Cesare didn't like the sound of those words. He had a sudden surge of irrational jealousy for this unknown employer. He glanced back at the stroller. And who was this baby?

He said only, "I'll pay double what you're paid now."

Emma's eyes hardened. "We've already had

this conversation, haven't we? I won't work for you at any price. It's not a question of money. We want different things. And we always will. You made that painfully clear to me in London."

The dark-haired baby gave an unhappy whimper from the stroller. Going down on one knee, she grabbed a pacifier from a big canvas bag and gave it to the baby, who instantly cheered up. She looked at the plump-cheeked, dark-eyed baby, then slowly rose to her feet, facing Cesare.

"Don't come looking for me again. Because nothing is going to change. And all you will bring us—all of us—is unhappiness."

Who was this baby? The question pounded in his heart. Her employer's? Emma's? But he couldn't ask. To ask the question would imply that he cared.

She stared at him for a moment, then turned away.

"I don't want you as my housekeeper," he said in a low voice. "The truth is…I miss you."

She looked back at him with an intake of breath, her lovely face stricken. She glanced at the baby in the stroller, who was simultaneously sucking like crazy on the pacifier, and trying to reach for his own feet. "I have other responsibilities now."

Cesare followed her gaze. The baby looked familiar somehow....

"I need a man I can trust. One I can count on to be permanent in my life. An equal partner. A father...for my baby."

For a moment, Cesare stared at her. Then as the meaning of her words sunk in, he literally staggered back. "*Your* baby?"

Emma nodded. Her eyes looked troubled, her expression filled with worry.

He could understand why.

"So much for all your big dreams," he ground out. "You left me for the wedding ring and the white picket fence." He couldn't control the bitterness in his voice as he flung his arm toward her bare left hand. "Where is your ring?"

"My baby's father didn't want to marry me," she said quietly.

"So you gave yourself away to some playboy? Someone who couldn't even give what I offered?" Jealousy raced through him. Once again, the woman he'd wanted, the one he'd chosen—had thrown herself away on another man. His hands curled into fists and he took a deep breath, regaining control. "I thought better of you." He lifted his chin. "So who is the father? Let me guess. Your new boss?"

"No," she said in a low voice. Slowly she lifted her eyes to his. "My old one."

He snorted. "Your old—"

Cesare gave an intake of breath as he looked down at the chubby black-haired baby.

I don't need a wedding proposal. He heard the echo of her trembling voice from long ago. *Or for you to say you're ready to be a father. I just need to know you might want those things someday. That you might be open to the possibility... if something ever...*

And he'd told her no. Flat-out. *Either this is a fun diversion, a friendship with benefits, or it's nothing.*

I'm going to have a baby, she'd said then. He'd thought she was trying to pin down his future. He hadn't realized she'd been talking about the present.

Cesare stared down at the baby's familiar black eyes—the same eyes he looked at every day in the mirror—and his knees nearly gave way beneath him.

"It's me," he breathed. "I'm the father."

CHAPTER FIVE

EMMA'S HEART POUNDED as she waited for Cesare's reaction.

She couldn't believe this was happening. For the past ten months, she'd dreamed of this. She'd thought of him constantly as their baby grew inside her. The day Sam was born. And every day since.

But now, she was afraid.

Alain Bouchard had been a wonderful boss to Emma, looking out for her almost like a brother through the months of her pregnancy and the sleepless nights beyond. But Alain hated Cesare, his former brother-in-law, blaming him for his sister Angélique's death. For ten months, Emma had waited for this day to come, for Cesare to find out about the baby—and the identity of her employer.

Over the past year, as she walked through the streets of Paris doing Alain's errands, shopping for fresh fruit and meats in the outdoor market on the Rue Cler, whenever she'd seen a tall, broad-shouldered, dark-haired man, she held her breath. But it was never Cesare. He hated Paris. It was partly why she'd chosen this job.

So today, when she'd seen a tall, dark-haired man pacing across the park, looking around with a strange desperation, she'd forced herself to ignore her instincts, because they were always wrong. She'd simply sat on the bench as her baby dozed in his stroller, and felt the warmth of the September sun on her skin. It had been almost a year since she'd last seen Cesare's face, since she'd last felt his touch. So much had happened. Their baby was no longer a tiny newborn. Sam had grown into a roly-poly four-month-old who could sleep seven hours at a stretch and loved to smile and laugh. Already, she could see his Italian heritage in his black eyes, the Falconeri blood.

But still, as Emma sat in the park, she hadn't been able to look away from the dark-haired man in a tailored suit, who seemed out of place as he stomped down the path, gulping down a coffee.

She'd told herself her imagination was working overtime. It absolutely *was not* Cesare.

Then he'd walked past her, barking into his cell phone. She saw his face, heard his voice. And time stood still.

Then, without thought, she'd reacted, leaping to her feet, calling his name.

Now, as she looked up at him, the world seemed to spin, the tourists and trees and dark outline of the Eiffel Tower a blur against the sky. There was Cesare. Only Cesare.

For so long, she'd craved him, heart and soul. Cried for him at night, for the awful choice she'd had to make. He'd told her outright he didn't want a child, but she'd still struggled with whether she'd made an unforgivable mistake, not telling him. Twice she'd even picked up the phone.

Now he was just inches away from her, close enough to touch. All throughout their conversation, she'd glanced at their baby out of the corner of her eye. How could he not instantly see the resemblance? How could he not see little Sam in the stroller, and *know?*

Well, Cesare knew now.

"I'm the father," he breathed, looking from Sam to her.

"Yes." Emma felt a thrill in her heart even as a chill of fear went down her spine. "He's yours."

Cesare's dark eyes were shocked, his voice hoarse. "Why didn't you tell me?"

"I…"

"How could you not tell me?" Pacing back two steps, he clawed back his dark hair. Whirling back to face her, he accused, "You knew you were pregnant when you left London."

She nodded. His dark eyes were filled with fury.

"You lied to me."

"I didn't exactly lie. I said I was going to have a baby…."

He sucked in his breath, then glared at her. "I thought you meant *someday.* And you let me believe that. So *you lied.*"

She licked her lips. "I wanted to tell you…"

"You were never on the Pill."

"I never said I was!"

His eyes narrowed. "You said—"

"I said I couldn't get pregnant," she cut him off. "I didn't think I could. When I was a teenager,

I was—very sick—and my doctor said future pregnancy might be difficult, if not impossible. I never thought I could…" She lifted her gaze to his and whispered, "It's a miracle. Can't you see that? Our baby is a miracle."

"A miracle." Cesare glowered at her. "And you never thought you should share the miracle with me?"

"I wanted to. More than you can imagine." Emma set her jaw. "But you made it absolutely clear you didn't want a family."

"Did you get pregnant on purpose?" he demanded. "To force me to marry you?"

Emma couldn't help herself. She laughed in his face.

"Why are you laughing?" he said dangerously.

"Oh, I'm sorry. I thought you were making a joke."

"This isn't a joke!"

"No. It isn't. But *you* are!" she snapped, losing patience.

He blinked as his mouth fell open.

She took a deep calming breath, blowing a tendril of hair off her hot forehead. "I've gone out of my way not to trap you. I'm raising this baby completely on my own. I wouldn't marry you even if you asked me!"

"Really?"

She stiffened, remembering that she had indeed once yearned to marry him—even hinted at it aloud! Her cheeks burned with humiliation. She lifted her chin. "Maybe once I was stupid enough to want that, but I've long since realized you'd make a horrible husband. No sane woman would want to marry a man like you."

"A man like me," he repeated. He looked irritated. "So you'd rather be a housekeeper, slaving for wages, instead of a billionaire's wife?" He snorted. "Do you really expect me to believe that?"

She glared back at him. "And do *you* really believe I'd want to sell myself to some man who doesn't love me, when I can support myself and my child through honest work?"

"He's not just your child."

"You don't want him. You said so in London. Right to my face."

"That was different. You made it sound like a choice. You didn't tell me the decision was already made." He folded his arms, six feet three inches of broad-shouldered masculine stubbornness. "I want him tested. To have DNA evidence he's my child."

She ground her teeth. "You don't believe me?"

"The woman who swore she couldn't get pregnant? No."

Ooh. She stamped her foot. "I'm not having Sam pricked with a needle for some dumb DNA test. If you don't believe me, if you think I might have been sleeping around and now I'm lying just for kicks, then forget about us. Just leave. We'll do fine without you."

He clenched his hands at his sides. "You should have told me!"

"I tried to, but when I started hinting at the idea of a child, you nearly fainted with fear!"

"I absolutely did *not* faint—" he began furiously.

"You did! From the moment I found out I was pregnant, I wanted to tell you. Of course I wanted to tell you. What do you take me for? My parents were married straight out of high school and loved each other until my mom died. That's what people do in my hometown. Get married and stay married. Buy a home and raise a family. Do you honestly think—" Emma's voice grew louder, causing nearby people in the park to look at them "—that I wanted to be a single mother? That this is something I *chose?*"

Cesare looked astonished, his sensual lips slightly parted, his own tirade forgotten. Then he scowled.

"Don't even try to—"

"Even now," she interrupted, feeling the tears well up, "when I've just told you you're a father, what are you doing? You're yelling at me, when any other man on earth would be interested in—I don't know—meeting his new *son!*"

He stopped again, staring at her, his mouth still open. Then he snapped it shut. He glared at her. "Fine."

"Fine!"

Cesare turned to the baby. He knelt by the stroller. He looked into Sam's chubby face. As Emma watched, his eyes slowly traced over the baby's dark eyes; exactly like his own. At the same dark hair, already starting to curl.

"Um," he said, awkwardly holding out a hand toward the baby. "Hi."

The baby continued to suck the pacifier, but

flung an unsteady hand toward his father. One little pudgy hand caught his finger. Cesare's eyes widened and his expression changed. He moved closer to Sam, then gently stroked his hair, his plump cheek. His voice was different as he said more softly, "Hi."

Seeing the two of them together, Emma's heart twisted.

"You named him Sam?" he asked a moment later.

"After my dad."

"He looks just like me," Cesare muttered. Pulling away from the baby, he rose to his feet. "Just tell me one thing. If I hadn't come to Paris, if I hadn't seen you today—would you ever have told me?"

She swallowed.

"You really are unbelievable," he ground out.

"You don't want a family." Her voice trembled. "All you could have given him was money."

"And a *name*," he flung out.

"He already has both." She looked at him steadily. "I've given him a name—Samuel Hayes. And I earn enough money. Not for mansions and private jets, but enough for a comfortable home. We don't need you. We don't want you."

Cesare ground his teeth. "You're depriving him of his birthright."

She snorted. "Birthright? You mean you'd have insisted on sending him to a fancy school and buying him something extravagant and useless at Christmas, like a pony, before you ignored him the rest of the year?" She shook her head. "And that's the best-case scenario! Because let's not pretend you actually want to be in the picture!"

"I might…" he protested.

"Oh, please." Her eyes narrowed. "All you could have offered was money and heartbreak. Better no father at all than a father like you. My child will never feel like an ignored, unwanted burden." She straightened her shoulders, lifting her chin. "And neither will I."

Cesare stared at her. Then his mouth snapped shut.

"So that's what you think of me," he muttered. "That I'm a selfish bastard with nothing but money to offer."

She stared at him for a long moment, then relented with a sigh. "You are who you are. I realized last year that I could not change you. So I'm not going to try."

His handsome face looked suddenly haggard. In spite of everything, her traitorous heart went out to him. Living with him for seven years, learning his every habit, she'd seen glimpses of the vulnerability that drove Cesare to a relentless pursuit of money and women he neither needed nor truly wanted. When he came home late at night, when he paced the hallways in sleepless hours, she'd seen flashes of emptiness beneath his mask, and the despair beneath his careless charm. There could never be enough money or cheap affairs to fill the emptiness in his heart, but he kept trying. And Emma knew why.

He'd lost the woman he'd loved, and he'd never be able to love anyone again.

Even through her anger, she felt almost sorry for him. Because without love, what could there be—but emptiness?

"It's not your fault," she said slowly. "I understand why you can't let anyone into your heart again. You loved her so much—and then you lost her..." At his expression, she reached her hand to his rough cheek. Her voice trembled as she whispered, "Your heart was buried with your wife."

Cesare seemed to shudder beneath her touch. "Emma…"

"It's all right." Dropping her hand, she stepped back and tried to smile. "We're fine. Truly. Your son is happy and well. I have a good job. My boss is a very kindhearted man. He looks out for us."

Something in her voice made him look up sharply.

"Who is he? This new boss?"

She licked her lips. "You don't know?"

He shook his head. "After you left, I tried my best to forget you ever existed."

It shouldn't have hurt her, but it did. Emma put her hands on the handlebar of the stroller. "That is what you should do now, Cesare. Forget us…."

But he grabbed the handlebar, his hand over hers. "No. This time, I'm not letting you go. Not with my son."

She swallowed, looking up at his fierce gaze.

"You only want us because you think you can't have us. *No* is a novelty, it's distracting and shiny. But I know, if I ever let myself…count on you,

you'd leave. I won't let anyone hurt Sam. Not even you."

She tried to pull away. He tightened his grip.

"He's my son."

"Let us go," she whispered. "Please. Somewhere, there's a man who will love us with all his heart. A man who can actually be a loving father to Sam." She shook her head. "We both know you're not that man."

The anger in Cesare's face slid away, replaced by an expression that seemed hurt, even bewildered.

"Emma," he breathed. "You think so little of me—"

"You heard her," a man growled behind them. "Let her go, damn you."

Alain Bouchard stood behind them with two bodyguards.

Cesare's eyes widened in shock. "Bouchard...?"

Alain was a powerful man, handsome in his way. In his mid-forties, he was a decade older than Cesare. His salt-and-pepper hair was closely clipped, his clothing well-tailored. His perfect posture bespoke the pride of a man who was CEO of a luxury goods firm that had been run by the Bouchard family for generations. But the red hatred in the Frenchman's eyes was for Cesare alone.

"Let her go," Alain repeated, and Emma saw his two burly bodyguards, Gustave and Marcel, take a step forward in clear but unspoken threat.

For an instant, Cesare's grasp tightened on her hand. His eyes narrowed and she was suddenly afraid of what he might do—that a brutal, juvenile fistfight between two wealthy tycoons might break out in the Champ de Mars.

Desperate to calm the situation down, she said, "Let me go, Cesare. Please."

He turned to her, his black eyes flints of betrayed fury. "What is he doing here?"

"He's my boss," she admitted.

"You work for Angélique's brother?"

She flinched. Strictly speaking, that might seem vengeful on her part. "He offered me a job when I needed one. That's all."

"You're raising my son in the house of a man who hates me?"

"I never let him speak a word against you. Not in front of Sam."

"That's big of you," he said coldly.

She saw Gustave and Marcel draw closer across the green grass. "Please," she whispered, "you have to let me go…."

Cesare abruptly withdrew his hand. There was a lump in Emma's throat as she turned away, quickly pushing the baby stroller toward Alain.

"Are you all right, Emma?" Alain said. "He didn't hurt you?"

Out of the corner of her eye, she saw Cesare stiffen.

"Of course I'm all right. We were just talking." She glanced behind her. "But now we're done."

"This isn't over," Cesare said.

His handsome face looked dark as a shadow crossed the sun. She took a deep breath. "I know," she said miserably.

"Allons-y," Alain said, putting a hand on the stroller handle, just where Cesare's had been a moment before. They walked together down the path and out of the park, and at every step, she felt Cesare's gaze on the back of her neck. She didn't properly breathe until they were out of the Champ de Mars and back on the sidewalk by the street.

"Are you really all right?" Alain asked again.

"Fine," she said. But she wasn't. A war was coming. A custody war with her precious baby at the center. She could feel it like the dark clouds of a rising storm. Trying to push aside her fear, she asked, "What were you doing at the park? How did you know we were there?"

"Gustave called me."

Her brow furrowed. "How did Gustave know?"

Alain's cheeks colored slightly. "I sometimes have my bodyguards watch you, at a distance. Paris can be a dangerous city…"

His voice trailed off as they were passed by two elegant women dripping diamonds and head-to-toe Hermès.

"This neighborhood?" Emma said in disbelief.

He gave a graceful Gallic shrug. *"On ne sait jamais."* His expression darkened. "And it seems I was right to have you followed, with that bastard Falconeri showing up. He's Sam's father, isn't he?"

She was sure he meant to be protective, but her privacy felt invaded. "Yes," she admitted. "But I don't blame him for being upset. I never told him I was pregnant."

"You obviously had reason. Is he going to try to take the baby?"

"I don't know," she said in a small voice.

"I won't let him." He stopped, looking down at her with his thin face and soulful eyes. "I'd do anything to protect you, Emma. You must know that."

She looked at her boss uneasily. "I know." In spite of all his kindness, she'd found herself wondering lately if he might be more interested in her than was strictly proper for an employer. She'd told herself she was imagining things. But still… She shook her head. "We'll be fine. I can take care of us."

Ahead, she saw Alain's black limited-edition Range Rover parked illegally on the Avenue de la Bourdonnais, with his chauffeur running the engine.

"After what he did to my sister, I won't let any woman be hurt by Cesare Falconeri, ever again," Alain vowed. Emma stiffened.

"Cesare didn't do anything to her. It was a tragic accident. He loved her."

"Ah, but you think the best of everyone." His expression changed from rage to gentleness as he looked down at her. His jaw tightened. "Even him. But that bastard doesn't deserve you. He'll get what he deserves. Someday."

Looking at him, Emma's heart trembled at what she might have unthinkingly done by accepting a job with Alain. He was convinced that his sister's death had been something more than a tragic accidental overdose. But Cesare was innocent. He'd never been charged with any crime. And Emma, of all people, knew how he'd loved his wife. She took a deep breath and changed the subject.

"Sam and I will be fine," she said brightly. "Cesare doesn't want a family to tie him down. He'll soon return to London and forget all about us."

But as dark clouds crossed the bright sun, Emma thought of the tender expression on Cesare's face when he'd first caressed his baby son's cheek. And she was afraid.

"To the airport, sir?"

Cesare leaned back heavily in the backseat of the Rolls-Royce. For a moment he didn't answer the driver. He pressed his hands against his forehead, still trembling with shock and fury from what he'd learned.

He had a child.

A son.

A baby born in secret, to the woman who'd left him last November without a word. And gone to work for his enemy.

Closing his eyes, he pressed his fingertips against the lids. He didn't believe Emma had gotten pregnant on purpose. No. She'd been right to laugh at his knee-jerk reaction earlier. She was clearly no gold digger. But leaving him in London, without a word, taking his child away, taking his *decision* away...

He took a deep breath. She'd done it all as if Cesare didn't even matter. As if he didn't even *exist*.

"Sir?"

"Yes," he bit out. "The airport."

The limousine pulled smoothly back into the Paris traffic. Cesare's throat was tight. He struggled to be fair, to be calm, when what he wanted to do was punch the seat in front of him and scream.

His baby was being raised in the house of Alain Bouchard, a man who unfairly blamed him for his sister's death. Bouchard didn't know the truth, and knowing how the man had loved his sister, Cesare had kept it that way.

But now, he pictured Bouchard's angry face, the way he'd stepped protectively in front of Emma.

Was it possible that over the past year, while Cesare had been celibate as a monk hungering for her, Emma had become Bouchard's lover?

No, his heart said. Impossible. But his brain disagreed. After all, the two of them were living in the same house. Perhaps she'd been lonely and heartsick. Perhaps he'd found her crying in the kitchen, as Cesare once had, and she'd fallen into the other man's bed, as she'd once fallen into his.

He hopelessly put his hands over his ears, as if that could keep his own imagination away. Anger built inside Cesare, rising like bile in his soul.

As the car turned west, heading toward the private airport outside the city, he looked out the window. He could see the top of the Eiffel Tower above the charming buildings, over two young lovers kissing at a sidewalk café.

He ground his teeth. He'd be glad to leave this damn city. He hated Paris and everything it stood for. The romance. The *love.*

Whether Emma was Bouchard's mistress or

not, she had no love for Cesare anymore. She'd
made her low opinion of him, as a potential father
or even as a human being, very clear. She didn't
want a thing from him. Not even his money. The
thought made him feel low.

It would be simple to take the easy out she offered. Leave Paris. Go back to London. Forget
the child they'd unintentionally created.

His child.

He could still see the baby's face. His soft black
hair. Those dark eyes, exactly like his own.

He had a son.

A child.

He closed his eyes. Over the memory of the
baby's sweet babble, he heard Emma's voice: *We
don't need you. We don't want you.*

Cesare's fist hit the window with a bang.

"Sir?" His driver quivered, looking at him in
the rearview mirror.

Cesare's eyes slowly opened. Perhaps he wasn't
ready to be a father. But that no longer mattered.

Because he was one.

"Go back."

"Back?"

"To my hotel." Cesare rubbed at the base of his skull. "I'm not leaving Paris. Take me back now."

Pulling his phone from his pocket, he dialed a number in New York City. Mortimer Ainsley had been his uncle's attorney, twenty years ago, and presided over his will when he'd died and Cesare gained possession of his aging, heavily mortgaged hotel. Later, Mortimer Ainsley had looked over the prenuptial agreement given to Cesare by Angélique Bouchard, the wealthy older French heiress who had proposed after just six weeks.

Morty, who'd appeared old to Cesare's eyes even then, had harrumphed over the terms of Angélique's prenup. "If you leave this Bouchard woman, you get nothing," he'd said. "If she dies, you get everything. Not much of a deal for you. She's only ten years older so it may be some time before she dies!"

Cesare had been horrified. "I don't want her to die. I love her."

"Love, huh?" Morty had snorted. "Good luck with that."

Remembering how young and naive he'd been, Cesare waited for Morty to answer the phone. He knew the old man would answer, no matter what time it was in New York right now. Morty would know the right attorney in Paris to handle a custody case.

Better no father at all than a father like you.

Cesare's jaw tightened. Emma would realize the penalty for what she'd done. She'd see that Cesare Falconeri would not be ignored, or denied access—or even knowledge!—of his own child.

"Ainsley." Morty's greeting was gruff, as if he'd just woken from sleep.

"Morty. I have a problem…." Without preamble, Cesare grimly outlined the facts.

"So you have a son," Morty said. "Congratulations."

"I told you. I don't have a son," Cesare said tightly. "*She* has him."

"Of course you can go to war over this. You might even win." Morty cleared his throat. "But you know the expression, *Pyrrhic victory?* Unless the woman's an unfit mother…"

Cesare remembered Emma's loving care of the baby as she pushed him in the stroller through the park. "No," he said grudgingly.

"Then you have to decide who you're willing to hurt, and how badly. 'Cause in a custody war, it's never just the other parent who takes it in the neck. Nine times out of ten, it's the kid who suffers most." Morty paused. "I can give you the number of a barracuda lawyer who will cause the sky to rain fire on this woman. But is that what you really want?"

As his Rolls-Royce crossed the Seine and traveled up the Avenue George V, Cesare's grip on his phone slowly loosened. By the time he ended the call a few minutes later, as the car pulled in front of the expensive five-star hotel where he'd stayed through the business negotiations, Cesare's expression had changed entirely.

The valet opened his door. "Welcome back, monsieur."

Looking up, Cesare didn't see the imposing architecture of the hotel as he got out. Instead he saw Emma's troubled expression when they'd parted in the Champ de Mars.

She was expecting him to start a war over this. *Christo santo,* she knew him well. Now that he knew about Sam, she expected him to fight for custody, to destroy their peace and rip their comfortable life into shreds. And then after that, after he'd made a mess of their lives for the sake of his pride, she expected Cesare to grow bored and quickly abandon them both.

That was why she hadn't told him about the baby. That was why she thought Sam was better off with no father at all. She truly believed Cesare was that selfish. That he'd put his own ego over the well-being of his child.

His lips pressed into a thin line. He might have done it, too, if Morty hadn't made him think twice.

You have to decide who you're willing to hurt, and how badly. 'Cause in a custody war, it's never just the other parent who takes it in the neck. Nine times out of ten, it's the kid who suffers most.

Before his own parents died, Cesare'd had a happy, almost bohemian childhood in a threadbare villa on Lake Como, filled with art and light and surrounded by beautiful gardens. His parents, both artists, had loved each other, and they'd adored their only child. The three of them had been inseparable. Until, when he was twelve, his mother had gotten sick, and her illness had poisoned their lives, drop by drop.

His father's death had been quicker. After his

wife's funeral, he'd gone boating on the lake in the middle of the night, after he'd drunk three bottles of wine. Calling his death by drowning an *accident,* Cesare thought, had been generous of the coroner.

Now his hands tightened. If he didn't go to war for custody, how else could he fulfill his obligation to his son? He couldn't leave Sam to be raised by another man—especially not Alain Bouchard. Sam would grow up believing Cesare was a monster who'd callously abandoned him.

Cesare exhaled.

How could he bend Emma to his will? What was the fulcrum he could use to gain possession of his child? What was her weakness?

Then—*he knew.*

And if some part of him shivered at the thought, he stomped on it as an irrational fear. This was no time to be afraid. This time, he wouldn't be selling his soul. There would be no delusional *love* involved. He would do this strictly for his child's sake. *In name only.*

He had a sudden image of Emma in his bed, luscious and warm, naked in his arms....

No! He would keep her in his home, but at a

distance. *In name only,* he repeated to himself. He would never open his heart to her again. Not even a tiny corner of it.

From this moment forward, his heart was only for his son.

Grabbing the car door as it started to pull away, he wrenched it open and flung himself back into the Rolls-Royce.

"Monsieur?"

"I changed my mind."

"Of course, sir," replied the driver, who was well accustomed in dealing with the inexplicable whims of the rich. "Where may I take you?"

Emma expected a battle. He would give her one. But not in the way she expected. He would take her completely off guard—and sweep her completely into his power, in a revenge far sweeter, and more explosive, than any mere *rain of fire.*

"Around the corner," Cesare replied coldly. "To a little jewelry shop on the Avenue Montaigne."

CHAPTER SIX

EMMA JUMPED WHEN her phone rang.

All afternoon, since she'd left Cesare in the park, she'd been pacing the halls of Alain's seventeenth-century *hôtel particulier* in the seventh arrondissement. She'd been on edge, looking out the windows, past the courtyard gate onto the Avenue Rapp. Waiting for Cesare to strike. Waiting for a lawyer to call. Or the police. Or... She didn't know what, but she'd been torturing herself trying to imagine.

When her cell phone finally rang, she saw his private number and braced herself.

"I won't let you bully me," she whispered aloud to the empty air. Then she answered the phone with, "What do you want?"

"I want to see you." It shocked her how calm Cesare's voice was. How pleasant. "I'd like to discuss our baby."

"I'm busy." Standing in the mansion's lavish salon with its fifteen-foot-high ceilings, she looked from the broom she hadn't touched in twenty minutes to Sam, lying nearby on a cushioned blanket on the floor, happily batting at soft toys dangling above him in a baby play gym. She set her jaw. "I'm working."

"As mother of my heir, you don't need to work, you know." He sounded almost amused. "You won't worry about money ever again."

He was trying to lull her into letting down her guard, she thought.

"I don't worry about money *now,*" she retorted. As a single mother, she'd been even more careful, tucking nearly all her paycheck into the bank against a rainy day. "I have a good salary, we live rent-free in Alain's house and I have a nice nest egg thanks to you. I sold your watch to a collector, by the way. I couldn't believe how much I got for it. What kind of idiot would spend so much on a— Oh. Sorry. But seriously. How could you spend so much on a watch?"

But Cesare didn't sound insulted. "How much did you get for it?"

"A hundred thousand euros," she said, still a little horrified. But also pleased.

He snorted. "The collector got a good deal."

"That's what Alain said. He was irritated I didn't offer the watch to him first. He said he would have paid me three times that.…" She stopped uneasily.

"Bouchard takes good care of you."

Cesare's good humor had fled. She gritted her teeth. What was the deal between those two? She wished they'd leave her out of it. "Of course Alain takes care of me. He's an excellent employer."

"You can't raise Sam in his house, Emma. I won't allow it."

"You won't allow it?" She exhaled with a flare of nostril. "Look, I told you that Sam's your child because it was the right thing to do…"

"You mean because I gave you no choice."

"…but you can't give orders anymore. In case you haven't noticed, you're no longer my boss."

His voice took on an edge. "I'm Sam's father."

"Oh, you're suddenly sure about that now, are you?"

"Emma—"

"I can't believe you asked me for a paternity test! When you know perfectly well you're the only man I've ever slept with in my whole life!"

"Even now?"

His voice was a little tense. Cesare was worried she'd slept with other men over the past year? She was astonished. "You think I was madly dating while I was pregnant as a whale? Or maybe—" she gave a low laugh "—right after Sam was born, I rushed to invite men to my bed, hoping they'd ignore the dark hollows under my eyes and baby spit-up on my shoulder." She snorted. "I'm touched, really, that you think I'm so irresistible. But if I have a spare evening I collapse into bed. For sleeping, not orgies, in case that was your next question."

For a moment, there was silence. When next he spoke, his tone was definitely warmer. "Leave Sam at home with a babysitter. Come out with me tonight."

"Why?" She scowled. "What do you have planned—the guillotine? Pistols at dawn? Or let me guess. Some lawyer is going to serve me a subpoena?"

"I just want to talk."

"Talk," she said doubtfully.

"Perhaps I was a little rough with you in the park…."

"You think?"

He gave a low laugh. "I don't blame you for believing the worst of me. But I'm sure you'll forgive my bad manners, when you think of what a shock it was for me to learn I have a son, and that you'd hidden that fact from me for quite some time."

He sounded reasonable. Damn him.

"What's your angle?" she asked suspiciously.

"I just want us to share dinner," he said, "and discuss our child's future. Surely there is nothing so strange in that."

Uh-oh. When Cesare sounded innocent, she *knew* he was up to something. "I'm not giving up custody. So if that's what you want to discuss, we should let our lawyers handle it." She tried to sound confident, like she even *had* a lawyer.

"Oh, *lawyers*." He gave a mournful sigh. "They make things so messy. Let's just meet, you and me. Like civilized people."

She gripped the phone tighter, pacing across the gleaming hardwood floors. "If you're thinking of luring me out of the house so your body-guards can try to kidnap Sam, Alain's house is like a fortress...."

"If you're going to jump to the worst possible conclusion of everything I say, this conversation is going to take a long time. And I wouldn't mind a glass of wine," he said pointedly.

She watched her baby gurgle with triumph when he caught the end of his sock. Falconeri men were such determined creatures. "You're not going to try to pull anything?"

"Like what?" When she didn't answer, he gave an exaggerated sigh. "I'll even take you some-place crowded, with plenty of strangers to chap-erone us. How about the restaurant at the top of the Eiffel Tower?"

She pictured the long circling queues of tour-ists. Surely even Cesare couldn't be up to much, amid such a crowd. "Well..."

"You left London without a word. You kept your pregnancy secret and went to work for Bouchard behind my back. I don't think a single dinner to work out Sam's custody is too much to ask."

Emma was about to agree when her whole body

went on alert at the word *custody*. "What do you mean, custody?"

"I'm willing to accept your pregnancy was an accident. You didn't intentionally lie. You're not a gold digger."

"Gee, thanks."

"But now I know I have a son, I can't just walk away. We're going to have to come to an arrangement."

"What arrangement?"

"If you want to know, you'll have to join me tonight."

"Or else—what?"

"Or else," Cesare said quietly. "Let's just leave it at that."

"You don't want to be a father," she said desperately. "You couldn't be a decent one, even if you tried—not that you would try for long!"

For a moment, the phone fell silent.

"You think you know me," he said in a low voice.

"Am I wrong?"

"I'll pick you up at nine." There was a dangerous sensuality in his voice that caused a shiver down Emma's body. She suddenly remembered that Cesare had ways of making her agree to almost anything.

"Make it seven," she said nervously. "I don't want to be out too late."

"Have a curfew, do you?" he drawled. "He keeps tight hold on you."

"Alain doesn't have anything to do with—"

"And Emma? Wear something nice."

The line went dead.

The sun was setting over Paris, washing soft pink and orange light over the white classical facades of the buildings as Emma stood alone on the sidewalk of the Avenue Rapp. It was three minutes before seven. She'd dressed carefully, as requested, in a pink knit dress and a black coat.

She'd considered showing up in a T-shirt and jeans, just to spite him. Instead she spent more time this afternoon primping than she'd spent in a year. For reasons she didn't like to think about. For feelings she was trying to convince herself she didn't feel.

Emma had stopped wearing the severe chignon when she'd come to Paris. Now her black hair had been brushed until it shone, and fell tumbling down her shoulders. Her lipstick was the same raspberry shade as her dress. She was even wearing mascara to make her green eyes pop. She hoped.

No. She ground her teeth. She *didn't* hope. She absolutely didn't care what Cesare thought she looked like. She *didn't.*

It was only for Sam's sake she was meeting Cesare tonight. Where her own romantic dreams were concerned, she'd given up on him that cold, heartbreaking morning in London when he'd informed her he would never ever: 1. love her, 2. marry her or 3. have a child with her. He'd said it outright. What could you do with a man like that?

What indeed…

Emma shivered in her thin black wool coat, tucking her pink scarf more firmly around her neck. Pulling her phone out of her pocket, she glanced at the time: six fifty-eight.

She sighed, wondering why she'd bothered to be on time. Cesare would likely be half an hour late, as usual, and in the meantime she was standing out here looking like a fool as taxi drivers gawked at her standing on the sidewalk. She would have gone back to wait inside, except the bad blood between Alain and Cesare made her reluctant to allow the two men to meet.

She'd already tucked her baby son into bed, leaving him with Irene Taylor, the extremely capable young woman who until recently had been an au pair for the Bulgarian ambassador. Irene was bright, idealistic and very young. Emma had never been that young.

Her eye was caught by a flash of light. Looking up over the buildings, she could see the tip of the Eiffel Tower suddenly illuminated with brilliant sparkling lights. That meant it was seven o'clock. Her lips turned down. And just as she'd thought, Cesare was late. He'd never change....

"Buona sera, bella."

With an intake of breath, Emma turned to see Cesare on the sidewalk, looking devastatingly handsome in a long black coat.

"You're on time," she stammered.

"Of course."

"You're never on time."

"I am always on time when it matters to me."

Her cheeks turned hot. Feeling awkward, she looked right and left. "Where's your car?"

Cesare came closer. "It's a beautiful night. I

gave my driver the night off." He tilted his head. "Why are you waiting on the sidewalk? I would have come to get you."

"I didn't want to start World War III."

He snorted. "I don't hold any grudge against Bouchard."

She looked at him steadily. "He holds one against you. The things he has said…"

His eyes narrowed. "On second thought, perhaps you are right to separate us. I am starting to resent the way he's taken possession of something that should belong only to me."

Emma trembled at the anger in his dark eyes. He meant Sam. He had to mean Sam.

"You look beautiful tonight," he said huskily.

"Oh. Thanks," she said, suddenly shy. Cesare looked even more handsome than she remembered, and cripes, was that a tuxedo beneath his black coat? "So do you." Her cheeks flamed. "Er, handsome, I mean. Not that it matters," she added hastily, "because we're just going out to talk about our son…."

She stopped talking as he took her hand in his own. She felt the warmth of his palm against hers. He glanced at her high-heeled shoes. "Do you mind walking a few blocks?"

In this moment, it was hard for Emma to remember what pain felt like. Wordlessly she shook her head.

He smiled, an impossibly devastating smile, and her heart twisted in her chest. "Too bad. I would have offered to carry you."

Carry her? Against his chest? Her mouth went dry. She tried to think of a snappy comeback but her brain suddenly wasn't working quite right. His smile increased.

Still holding her hand, he led her across the street and up the narrow, charming rue de Monttessuy. The Eiffel Tower loomed large, directly ahead of them. But it wasn't that world-famous sight that consumed her.

She glanced down at Cesare's hand as they walked up the quiet street, past the brasseries and shops. He held her hand as if she were precious and he never wanted to let her go.

"Is something wrong, *cara?*"

Emma realized she'd stopped on the sidewalk right in front of the boulangerie. "Um…"

He pulled her closer, looking down at her with

dark intense eyes as his lips curved. "Perhaps you want me to carry you, after all?"

She swallowed.

Yes.

No.

She took a deep breath of air, scented with warm, buttery croissants and crusty baguettes, and reminded herself she wasn't in London anymore. She didn't love Cesare. She'd left that love behind her. He had no power over her here. None.

"Absolutely none," she whispered aloud.

Moving closer, he stroked her cheek. "None?"

She pulled away from him, trembling. "Why are you acting like this?"

"Like what?"

"Like you care."

"I do."

She shook her head, fighting tears. "I don't know what you're planning, but you—"

"Just dinner, Emma," he said quietly. "And a discussion."

"Nothing more?"

He gave her a lopsided grin that tugged at her heart. "Would I lie?"

"No," she sighed.

He pulled her across the Avenue de la Bourdonnais, which was still busy with early-evening traffic. They walked down the charming tree-lined street into the Champ de Mars, to the base of the Eiffel Tower. She exhaled when she saw the long lines of tourists. In spite of all his promises, she still almost feared Cesare might try something. Not seduce her, surely?

No, why would he?

Unless it was a cold-blooded calculation on his part. Unless he thought he could overwhelm her with sensuality until she was so crazy she agreed to give up custody of Sam. Her hands tightened at her sides. He wouldn't even get a single kiss out of her if he tried. And the next time he contacted her, she really would have a lawyer....

"Elevator or stairs?" he asked, smiling.

Tilting her head back to look up the length of the tower, Emma had a sudden image of tripping on the stairs in her high heels, and Cesare sweeping her up into his arms. She could almost imagine how it would feel to cling to him, her arms around his body, her cheek against his chest.

"Elevator," she said quickly.

They went to a private elevator at the south pillar of the Eiffel Tower. There was no queue here. *Strange,* she thought. She'd heard this restaurant was really popular.

She was even more shocked when the elevator opened with a ding on the second platform of the Eiffel Tower, and they walked into a beautiful restaurant…

And found it empty.

Emma stopped cold. With an intake of breath, she looked at Cesare accusingly. "Where is everyone?"

He shrugged, managing to look guilty and innocent at the same time. "What do you mean?"

She looked over all the empty tables and chairs of the modern restaurant, with its spectacular views of Paris from all sides. "No one is here!"

Coming behind her, he put his hands on her shoulders.

"*We* are here."

Slowly he pulled off her coat, then handed it to a host who discreetly appeared. Cesare's eyes never left hers as he removed his own coat, revealing his well-cut tuxedo. Emma shivered beneath his gaze for reasons that had nothing to do with being cold. As he led her to a table by the window, the one with the best view, she felt suddenly hot, as if she'd been lying beneath the sun. No, worse. As if she'd been *standing* on it.

They sat down, and a waiter brought them a bottle of wine. Emma glanced at the tables behind them and saw they were all covered with vases of long-stemmed roses.

"Roses?" she said. Her lips curled humorlessly. "To go along with the watch you gave me? The finishing touch on the parting-gift extravaganza for one-night stands?"

"I should think it's obvious," he drawled, pouring wine into her glass, "you're not a one-night stand."

"A two-night stand, then."

He looked at her without speaking. Her cheeks burned.

"I won't let you talk me into signing custody away," she said hoarsely. "Or seduce me into it, either."

He gave a low laugh. "Ah, you really do think I'm a coldhearted bastard." He held out her glass, filled with wine a deeper red than roses. "That's not what I want."

"Then, what?"

He just looked at her with his dark eyes. Emma's heart started pounding.

Her hand shook as she reached out for the glass. She realized she was in trouble. Really, really big trouble.

He held up his own wine. "A toast."

"To what?"

"To you, *cara*," he murmured.

He clinked her glass and then drank deeply. She looked down at the glass and muttered, "Should I wonder if this is poisoned?"

He gave a low laugh. "No poison, I promise."

"Then, what?" she whispered.

Cesare's dark eyebrow quirked. "How many times must I say it? I want to have *dinner*. And *talk*." He picked up the menu. "What looks good?"

"I'm not hungry."

"Not hungry? With a menu like this? There's steak—lobster…"

"Will you just stop torturing me with all this romantic nonsense and tell me why you've brought me here?"

He tilted his head, looking at her across the

table, before he gave a low laugh. "It's the roses, isn't it? Too much?"

"I'm not one of your foolish little starlets getting tossed out after breakfast, sobbing to stay." She narrowed her eyes. "You never try this hard. You never have to. So it must be leading up to something. Tell me what it is."

Cesare leaned forward across the candlelit table, his dark eyes intense. Her whole body was taut as she leaned toward him, straining to hear. He parted his sensual lips.

"Later," he whispered, then relaxed back in his chair as if he had not a care in the world. He took another sip of wine and looked out the huge wall of windows overlooking the lights of Paris, twinkling in the twilight.

Emma glared in helpless fury. He clearly was determined to take his own sweet time, to make her squirm. Fine. Grabbing her glass, she took a big gulp of the wine. Since she'd moved to Paris, she'd grown to appreciate wine more. This was a red, full-bodied Merlot that was equal parts delicious and expensive. Setting down her glass, she looked around them.

"This restaurant is kind of famous. It's hard to

even get reservations here. How on earth did you manage to get the whole place?"

He gave a low laugh. "I pulled some strings."

"Strings?"

"It wasn't easy."

"For you," she said darkly, "everything is easy."

"Not everything." He looked at her across the table. His eyes seemed black as a midnight sea. Then he looked past her. Turning around, she saw the waiter approaching their table.

"Monsieur?" the man asked respectfully. "May I take your order?"

"Yes. To start, I'd like…" Cesare rattled off a list that included endives, foie gras, black truffle sauce, venison and some kind of strange rose-flavored gelatin. It all sounded very fancy to Emma, and not terribly appetizing.

"And for madame?"

Both men looked at her expectantly.

Emma sighed. "I'm afraid I don't much care for French food."

The waiter did a double take. So did Cesare. The scandalized looks on both male faces was almost funny. Emma stifled a laugh.

"Of course you like French food," Cesare said.

"Everyone does. Even people who hate Paris love the food."

"I love Paris," she said. "Just not the food."

"I can give madame some suggestions from the menu…" the waiter tried.

She shook her head. "Sorry. I've lived here for almost a year. Trust me, I've tried everything." She looked at him. "What I would really like is a cheeseburger. With French fries. *Frites,*" she amended quickly, as if that would make her order sound more gourmet, which of course it didn't.

The waiter continued to stare at her with a mix of consternation and bewilderment. In for a penny, in for a pound.…

"And ketchup." She handed him the menu with a sweet smile. "Lots and lots of ketchup. *Merci.*"

The waiter left, shaking his head and muttering to himself.

But Cesare gave a low laugh. "Nice."

"Shouldn't I order what I want?" she said defensively.

"Of course you should. Of course a nice American girl, on a romantic night out at the Eiffel Tower, would order a cheeseburger with ketchup."

"Romantic night?" she said with a surge of

panic. He gave her an inscrutable smile. To hide her confusion, she looked out the window. "I can still enjoy the view."

"Me, too," he said quietly, and he wasn't looking at the window. A tingle of awareness went up and down Emma's body.

"This is my first time inside the Eiffel Tower," she said, trying to fill the space between them. She gave an awkward laugh. "I could never be bothered to wait in the lines."

"Doesn't Bouchard ever give you time off?"

She glanced at him with a snicker. "You're one to talk."

He had the grace to look discomfited. "I was a difficult boss."

"That," she said succinctly, "is an understatement."

"I must have been an awful employer."

"A monster," she agreed.

"You never even got to see inside the British Museum." He had a hangdog look, like a puppy expecting to be kicked. "Or take a picture of Big Ben."

She squelched an involuntary laugh, covering it with a cough. Then sighed.

"Perhaps you weren't entirely to blame," she admitted.

He brightened. "I wasn't?"

"I blamed you for not having time to tour London. I swore Paris would be different. But even though Alain has bent over backward to be the most amazing employer I could possibly imagine…"

Cesare's expression darkened.

"…I still haven't seen much of the city. At first, I was overwhelmed by a new job in a new city. Then I had the baby, and, well…if I have extra time, I don't tour a museum any more than I go on a date. I collapse in a stupor on the couch." She sighed, spreading her arms. "So it seems I'm full of excuses. I could have climbed the Eiffel Tower before now, and brought Sam with me, if I'd made it a priority. Instead I haven't been willing to wait in line or pay the money."

"What if I promised you'd never have to do either, seeing the sights of London?"

She tried to laugh it off. "What, there's no line to see the Crown Jewels anymore?" she said lightly. "It's a free ride for all on the London Eye?"

He took another sip of his wine, then put it back

down on the table. His dark eyes met hers. "I want you both to come back to London with me."

She set her jaw. She'd been afraid he'd say that. "There's no way I'm leaving my job to move back to London with you. Your interest in Sam will never last."

"You have to know I can't abandon him, now I know. Especially not in Bouchard's house."

"I thought you said you didn't bear Alain any grudge."

"I don't. But that doesn't mean I'll let him raise my son." The votive candle on the table left flickering shadows on the hard lines of his handsome face. He said quietly, "Bouchard wants you for himself, Emma."

"Don't be ridiculous," she said uncomfortably, then recalled her own recent concerns on that front. "And anyway, I don't see him that way."

"He wants you. And he already knows that taking care of Sam is the way to your heart." His voice was low. Behind him, she could see the sparkling lights of Paris in the night. "As you yourself said—Sam deserves a father."

"Yes, he does," she said over the lump in her throat. "An actual father who'll love him and kiss his bruises and tuck him in at night. A father he can count on." Looking up at him, she whispered, "We both know you're not that man."

"How do you know?"

The raw emotion in Cesare's voice made her eyes widen. She shook her head.

"You said yourself you don't want a child. You have no idea what it means to be a parent...."

"You're wrong. I do know. Even though I'm new at being a father, I was once a son." He looked away. "We had no money, just an old house falling down around us. But we were happy. My parents loved each other. And they loved me."

She swallowed. "I've never heard you talk about them before."

"There's not much to tell." His lips twisted down at the edge. "When I was twelve, my mother got sick. My father had to watch her slowly die. He couldn't face life without her, so after her funeral, he went drinking alone on the lake at night. The empty boat floated to shore. His body was found the next day."

"I'm sorry," she choked out, her heart in her throat. "How could he do that—leave you?"

"I got over it." He shrugged, his only sign of

emotion the slight tightening of his jaw. "I was sent to a great-uncle in New York. He was strict, but tried his best to raise me. I learned English. Learned about the hotel business. Learned I liked hard numbers, profit and loss. Numbers made sense. They could be added, subtracted, controlled. Unlike love, which disappears like mist as soon as you think it's in your arms."

His wife. He was still brokenhearted over his loss of her. Emma fought back tears as she said, "Love makes life worth living."

His lips twisted sardonically. "You say that, even after you wasted so many years trying to get love from your stepmother, like blood from a stone? All those years trying and failing, with nothing but grief to show for it."

Pain caught at her heart.

"I'm sorry," Cesare said, looking at her. "I shouldn't have said that."

"No. You're right." Blinking back tears, she shook her head. "But others have loved me. My parents. My mother died when I was four, even younger than you were. Ovarian cancer. Just like…" She stopped herself. *Just like I almost did,* she'd almost said.

"I'm sorry," he said.

"It's all right. It was a long time ago. And my father was an amazing man. After my mom died, it was just the two of us. He gave me my work ethic, my sense of honor, everything." She pressed her lips together. "Then he fell in love with a coworker at his factory...."

"Cruel stepmother, huh?"

"She was never cruel." She sobered. "At least not at first. I was glad to see my father happy, but I started to feel like I was in their way. An outsider interrupting their honeymoon." She glanced up at the waiter, who'd just brought their meals. He set the cheeseburger and fries before her with the same flourish he used on Cesare's venison and risotto with black truffle sauce. It must have been hard for him, she thought, so she gave him a grateful smile. *"Merci."*

"So you left home?" Cesare prompted after the waiter left.

"Well." She dipped a fry into a ramekin of ketchup, then chewed it thoughtfully. It was hot and salty and delicious. She licked her lips, then her fingers. "At sixteen, I fell head over heels for a boy."

Cesare seemed uninterested in his own food as he listened with his complete attention. "A boy."

"The captain of the high school football team." She gave a smile. "Which in Texas can be a big deal. I was flattered by his attention. I fell hard. A few kisses, and I was convinced it was love. He talked me into going all the way."

"But you didn't." Taking a bite of his food, he grinned at her. "I know you didn't."

"No." She swirled another fry through the ketchup. "But I went to the doctor to get birth control pills." With a deep breath, she looked him in the eye. "That's how I found out I had cancer."

His jaw dropped. "Cancer?"

"Ovarian, the same as my mom had had." She kept stirring the fry in the ketchup, waiting for him to freak out, for him to look at her as if she still had one foot in the grave. "I was on chemotherapy for a long time. By the time I was in remission, Mark had long since dumped me for a cheerleader."

Cesare muttered something in Italian that sounded very unkind. She gave a grateful smile.

"He did me a huge favor. I'd had no symptoms. If I hadn't gone to the doctor then, I never would have known I was sick until it was too late. So in a funny way—that broken heart was the price that saved my life." She ate a bite of French fry, then made a face when she realized the bite was almost entirely ketchup. She set it down on her plate. "Though for a long time I wished I *had* died."

"Why?"

"My illness took everything. My childhood. My dreams of having a family someday. The medical bills even took our house." Her throat ached, but she forced herself to tell the worst. "And it killed my father."

Reaching across the table, he grabbed her hand. "Emma…"

She took a deep breath. "It was my fault. My father wasn't the kind of man who could declare bankruptcy and walk away from debt. So to pay all the bills, he took a night job. Between his jobs and taking care of me, he started to neglect my stepmother. They started fighting all the time. But the day my doctor announced I was in re-mission, I convinced my father to take me home early. It was Valentine's Day. I talked him into stopping at the florist to buy flowers. As a surprise." She paused. "Marion was surprised, all right. We found her at home, in bed, with the foreman from their factory."

Cesare sucked in his breath. "And?"

"My father had a heart attack," she whispered. She ran her hand over her eyes. "He was already so run-down from taking care of me. From working two jobs. Marion blamed me for everything." Her voice caught as she covered her face with her hands. "She was right."

His voice was gentle as he pulled back her hands. "It wasn't your fault."

"You're wrong." Emma looked at him across the table, and tears ran unchecked down her face. "If I hadn't fought so hard to live, I'd never have been such a burden. My father wouldn't have had to work two jobs, my stepmother wouldn't have felt lonely and neglected, and they'd still be together. It's my fault. I ruined their lives."

"Your stepmother said that?"

She nodded miserably. "After the funeral, she kicked me out of the house. I was eighteen. She had no legal obligation to take care of me. A friend let me stay until I graduated high school, then I left Texas for New York. I wanted to make something of myself, to prove Marion wrong." She blinked fast. "But nothing I ever did, not all the money I sent her, ever made her forgive what I did."

Rising to his feet, Cesare came around the table. Gently pulling Emma from the chair, he wrapped her in his arms. "So that's why you looked so stricken," he murmured. "The night we first… The night you came back from her funeral."

"Yes. Plus…" She swallowed. It was time to tell him the worst. To tell him everything. She thought of all her lonely years, loving him, devoting herself only to him. She looked up, barely seeing his face through her tears. "When I told you I loved you last year, you tried to convince me it was just lust. But there's a reason I knew all along that it wasn't." She took a deep breath and said, "I've loved you for years, Cesare."

His hands, which had been caressing her back, abruptly stopped. He looked down at her. "Years?"

"You never knew?"

Wide-eyed, he shook his head.

"I loved you from almost the first day we met,"

she said quietly. She gave a choked laugh. "I think it was the moment you said you were glad to have me, because I looked smart, and the previous housekeeper on the penthouse floor had just been fired for being idiot enough to fall for you."

He looked bewildered. "That made you love me?"

She gave a low laugh. "I guess you were wrong when you said I looked smart."

"I thought you had no feelings. I never knew…"

"I hid it even better than I thought." Her lips quirked. "I knew you would fire me if you ever guessed."

"But why? Why would you love me in silence for years? I ran roughshod over you. Bossed you around. Expected you to be at my beck and call."

"But I saw the rest, too," she said over the lump in her throat. "The vulnerability that drove you to succeed, as if the devil himself were chasing you. The way you were kind to children when you thought no one was looking. Giving money to charity, helping struggling families stay in their homes—anonymously. So no one would know."

He abruptly released her, pacing back a step in his tuxedo. His handsome face looked pale.

"But now." He took a deep breath, then licked his cruel, sensual lips. "But now, surely you don't...love me."

She saw the fear in his eyes.

"Don't worry," she said softly. "I got over loving you the day I left London. I knew we'd never have a future. I had to leave my broken heart behind me, to start a new life with my child."

For a moment he didn't reply. Then he pressed his lips together. "*Our* child."

"Yes." She sighed. She looked straight into his eyes, her heart aching as she said, "But not for long."

"What do you mean?"

"You won't last."

He stepped toward her. "You really think I would abandon him? After everything I've said?"

She matched him toe to toe. "I won't be a burden, or let Sam feel like one, either, wondering what's wrong with him that his own father can't be bothered to spend time with him." She lifted her chin, but as their eyes locked, she faltered.

"You're not a bad person, Cesare. But trying to raise him separately, together, it's just not going to work."

"So you can find some other man to raise my son."

Her eyes shone with tears as she whispered, "You can't promise forever. You know you can't. So if you have any mercy in your heart—if you truly do care for Sam—please, let us go."

His expression changed. He took a long, dragging breath.

"Everything you're saying," he said slowly, "is bull."

Her lips parted in a gasp.

Cesare glared at her. "You didn't keep the baby a secret because you were trying to protect me from this choice. You didn't do it to protect Sam, either. You did it for one person and one person only. Yourself."

"How can you say that?" she demanded.

"Are you honestly telling me that it's better for Sam to believe his own father abandoned him? Yes, I'm selfish. Yes, I work too much. Yes, it's possible I might buy him a pony. Maybe I wouldn't be a perfect father. But you wouldn't—won't—even give me a chance. It isn't Sam that you fear will be a burden." He looked at her. "*It's you.* You're afraid I will take charge of him, and you'll be left behind. You're afraid for yourself. *Only yourself.*"

Emma stared at him, her lips parted in shock. The accusation was like a knife in her heart.

Was he right? Could he be?

She shook her head fiercely.

"*No.* You're wrong!"

"You don't want to lose him," he growled. "Neither do I. From this moment, his needs must come first." He paused. "I did think of suing you for full custody…"

Those words were an ice pick in Emma's heart. She made a little whimpering sound. "No…"

"But a custody battle would only hurt my son. I'm not going to leave him in Bouchard's care, either. Or abandon him, whatever you say. I'm not going to shuttle a small child between continents, between two different lives. That leaves only one clear path. At least it's clear to me." Pulling a small jewelry box from his tuxedo pocket, he opened the box, revealing an enormous diamond ring.

"Emma Hayes," he said grimly, "will you marry me?"

CHAPTER SEVEN

CESARE STOOD BEFORE her, waiting for her answer. He hadn't even thought of bending down on one knee. His legs were shaking too badly. He was relieved his voice hadn't trembled at the question. The words felt like marbles in his mouth.

Hearing a soft gasp, he glanced behind him. Five members of the restaurant's staff were peeking from the kitchen door, smiling at this moment, waiting for Emma's answer, in that universal interest in the drama of a wedding proposal.

Will you marry me?

Four simple words. A promise that was easy to say, though not so easy to fulfill.

Cesare had the sudden memory of his father's bleak face after his beloved wife had died in his arms. The same look of stark despair on Angélique's face when Cesare had come home and found her dead, an empty bottle of sleeping pills on the floor beside her.

No. He wouldn't let himself remember. This was different. *Different.*

Cesare held the black jewelry box up a little higher, to disguise how his hand was shaking.

"Marry you?" Emma's eyes were shocked. Even horrified. She gave an awkward laugh. "Is this a joke?"

"You think I would joke about this?"

Biting her lip, she looked at the ring. "But you don't want to get married. Everyone on earth knows that, and from the day I've known you, every woman has tried to marry you anyway. We used to laugh about it."

"I'm not laughing now," he said quietly. "I'm standing in front of you with a twenty-carat ring. I don't know how much more serious I can be."

Her beautiful face looked stricken. "But you don't love me."

"It's not a question of love—at least not between us. It's a question of providing the best life for our son."

Her gaze shuttered, her green eyes filling with shadows in the flickering candlelight of the restaurant. She backed up one step—physically backed away—wrapping her arms across her body, as if for protection.

Nothing prepared him for what came next.

"I'm sorry, Cesare," she said quietly. "My answer is no."

He was so shocked, his hand tightened on the jewelry box, closing it with a snap. He'd assumed she would say yes. Instantly and gratefully.

He heard gasps behind him and whirled to face the restaurant staff hanging about the kitchen doorway.

"Leave us," he growled, and they ran back into the kitchen. He turned to face Emma, his jaw taut. "Might I ask—why?"

She swallowed. He saw her face was pale. This was hard on her, too, he realized. "I told you. I won't be a burden."

"Burden. You keep using that word. What does it mean?"

His dangerous tone would have frightened most. But standing her ground, she lifted her chin.

"You know what it means."

"No, I don't. I know you've lied to me for

months, that you stole my son away without a word. But instead of trying to take him away from you, instead of seeking revenge, I'm trying to do the right thing—a new experience for me, I might add—while you keep whining words like *love* and *burden*."

Her shoulders drooped as, biting her lip, she looked down. For a long moment, she didn't answer, and he looked at her in the darkness of the restaurant. She looked so beautiful in the flickering candlelight, with all of the lights of Paris at her feet.

Cesare's throat tightened.

He thought of the night he'd found her in the dark kitchen, after her stepmother's funeral. He'd taken one look at her tearstained face, at the anguish in eyes which had never shown emotion before, and his own long-buried grief had risen in his own soul, exploding through his defenses. He'd thought he was offering her solace, but the truth was that he'd been seeking it himself. Against his will, in that moment, Emma had made him *feel* again....

Now he heard her take a deep breath.

"Whatever you think now, this desire to commit won't last. You don't want the burden of a wife and child. We both know it. You don't know what marriage means."

"We both know I do," he said quietly.

Her eyes were anguished as tears sparkled—unheeded, unfought—down her cheeks like diamonds. "But you don't love me," she whispered again.

"And you don't love me," he said evenly. "Do you?"

Wordlessly she shook her head. He exhaled. "This marriage has nothing to do with romance."

She gave a half-hysterical laugh, swooping her arm to indicate the roses, the view of Paris, the twenty-carat diamond ring. "What do you call that?"

He gave her a crooked half grin. "I call it… strategic negotiation."

Emma gave another laugh, then her smile fell. "A marriage without love?"

"Without complications," he pointed out. "We will both love our son. But between us—the marriage will be in name only."

"In name only?" He'd shocked her with this.

He saw it in her face. "So you wouldn't expect us to…"

He shook his head. "Sex complicates things." Not to mention made it hard to keep the walls around his heart intact. At least where she was concerned. He hesitated. "Better that we keep this relationship…"

"Professional?"

"Cordial, I was going to say."

She took a deep breath.

"Why would I agree to give up any chance at love?"

"For something you want more than love," he said quietly. "For a family. For Sam."

"Sam…"

"I will love him. I'll be there with him every step of the way. Every single day. Isn't that better than trying to shuttle him between two separate lives, where he never knows where he belongs?"

Raw yearning filled her soft green eyes. Blinking fast, she turned away, to the dark, sparkling view of Paris. "I've worried about what would happen to Sam, if anything ever happened to me…" Looking up at him, she swallowed. "I've been in remission a long time, but there are no guarantees. If the cancer ever came back…" She looked up at him. "I've been selfish," she whispered. "Maybe you're right. Maybe even a flawed father is better than none."

"I will be the best father I can be."

"Would you?" she said in a small voice. Her beautiful face was tortured, her pink lips trembling, long dark lashes sweeping against pale cheeks. "Or, if I were crazy enough to accept, would you panic within a month and run off with some lingerie model?"

Coming toward her, he took both her hands in his own. "I swear to you, on my life," he said softly. "Everything your father was for you—I will be for him."

He felt her hands tremble in his.

"I won't let you break his heart," she whispered.

"I don't lie, and I don't make promises. You know that."

Her voice was barely audible. "Yes."

"I don't make promises because I consider myself bound by them." Gently he placed the black jewelry box with the silver Harry Winston logo into her palm. "I'm making you a promise now."

Her anguished eyes lifted to his. "Please…"

"You are the mother of my child. Be my wife." Brushing back long tendrils of black hair from her shoulder, he lowered his head to her ear. He took a deep breath, inhaling the scent of her. She smelled like vanilla and sunlight, like wildflowers and clean linen and everything good he'd once had but had lost so long ago. He felt a shudder of desire, but pushed it aside. He wouldn't let sex complicate this relationship. He couldn't. Pulling back, he said softly, "Be my wife, Emma."

Were her hands still trembling? Or were his?

"Cesare…." He saw how close she was to falling off the precipice. She tried, "We don't have to marry. We can live apart, but still raise Sam together…."

"In separate houses? In separate cities? Sending a small child with a little suitcase back and forth between two lives? You already said that wouldn't work. And I agree." Slowly, so slowly it almost killed him, he pulled her into the circle of his embrace, encircling her like a skittish thoroughbred into an enclosure. His gaze searched hers. "Marry me now. Take my name, and let my son be a Falconeri. I swear to you. On my life. That I will be the father you dreamed he could have."

She swallowed. "You swore you'd never get married again," she breathed. "We both know—" their eyes met "—you're still in love with your lost wife, and always will be."

He didn't deny this. It was easier not to.

"But we won't be lovers," he said. "We'll be equal partners." His fingers stroked her black hair, tumbling in glossy waves down her back. "And together—we'll raise our son."

She exhaled, visibly trying to steady herself. "For how long?"

"For always," he said in a low voice. "I will be married to you…until death do us part."

Her skin felt almost cold to the touch. He could almost feel her heart pounding through her ribs. "It would be a disaster."

"The only disaster would be to let any selfish dreams—yours or mine—destroy our son's chance for a home." Stroking down her cheek, he cupped her face. "Say you'll be my wife, Emma," he said huskily. "Say it."

Tears suddenly fell off her black lashes, trailing haphazardly down her pale cheeks.

"I can't fight you," she choked out. "Not when you're using my own heart against me. My baby deserves a father. It's all I've wanted since the day I found out I was pregnant." Her beautiful eyes were luminous with emotion, her body tense, as she stood in his arms in the rose-strewn restaurant of the Eiffel Tower, all the lights of Paris beneath them. "You win," she said. "I'll marry you, Cesare."

"Do you want me to come up with you?"

For answer, Emma shook her head, though she didn't let go of Cesare's hand. She hadn't let it go for the whole walk home from the Eiffel Tower. Her knees still felt weak. Now, as they stood outside Alain's gated courtyard, she was trembling. Possibly from the weight of the enormous diamond on her left hand.

Either that, or from the knowledge that she'd just thrown all her own dreams away, her precious dreams of being loved, for someone she loved more than herself: her son.

"Are you sure? Bouchard might not be pleased at the news."

"It will be fine." She still couldn't believe she'd

agreed to Cesare's marriage proposal. He'd loved only one woman—his long-dead wife—and would never love another. Knowing that, how could she have said yes?

But how could she not? He'd offered her everything she'd ever wanted for Sam. A home. A family. A real father, like she'd had. How could she not have made the sacrifice of something so small and inconsequential as her own heart?

At least she didn't need to worry about falling in love with Cesare again. She'd burned that from her soul. She *had*...

"You won't change your mind the instant I let you out of my sight?" he said lightly.

She shook her head.

"I think I'd better stay close, just to be safe." Cesare's voice was husky as he carefully tucked her jaunty pink scarf around her black coat. "Bouchard might try to talk you out of marrying me."

Even though she didn't love him anymore—*at all*—having Cesare so close did strange things to her insides. Emma took a deep breath. But she couldn't let herself feel anything. Not love. Not even lust. Not this time.

She was going to be his wife. In name only. She'd have to keep her distance, while living in the same house.

"Seriously, don't come," she said. She looked past the gate at Alain Bouchard's mansion. "I'd better give Alain this happy news on my own."

Cesare gave her a lopsided grin that made her heart go thump, thump in her chest. "I'll get the car, then. Meet you back here in ten minutes?"

"Ten?" she said incredulously.

"Twenty?"

"Better make it an hour. It's amazing how long it takes to pack up a baby."

"Really? He seems small."

"*He* is, but he has a lot of stuff." At his bemused expression, she snorted. "You'll learn."

"Can't wait." Pulling her close, Cesare looked down into her eyes. Cupping her face, he looked down at her one last time as they stood on the street with the lights of Paris twinkling around them. "Thank you for saying yes. You won't regret it."

"I regret it already," she mumbled, then gave a small laugh to show she was joking, holding up her left hand. "This diamond ring weighs, like, a thousand pounds. See you in an hour."

Turning, she went through the gate, past the security guard into Alain's courtyard. One of his personal bodyguards was waiting by the mansion door.

"Monsieur Bouchard is not happy with you, mademoiselle," Gustave said flatly.

She stopped. "Were you—following me?"

The man jutted his chin upward, toward the house. "He's waiting for you."

Emma had meant to tell Alain her news in the most gentle way possible. Instead it seemed he already had a good guess what was coming. Well, fine. She narrowed her eyes. He shouldn't have had her followed.

Going upstairs, she walked right past Alain's office, but not before she saw him scowling at his desk. First, she went to check on her baby, and found him sleeping in his crib. For a moment, she listened to his soft breath in the darkness. Tenderness and joy caught at her heart. Smiling to herself, she whispered aloud, "You're going to have a family, Sam. You're going to have a real dad."

Creeping out, she closed the door, and went to the next-door sitting room, where she found Irene Taylor reading tranquilly in an armchair.

"How was everything?" Emma asked.

"Oh, he was perfect. An angel." Smiling, Irene tucked her book, a romantic novel by Susan Mallery, carefully into her handbag. "Did you have a nice evening?"

Wordlessly Emma held out her left hand. Irene gasped, snatching up her hand and staring at the ring.

"Are you *kidding?*" She made a big show of rubbing her eyes. "Ah! It's blinding me!" She looked up at Emma with a big grin. "You sly girl, I didn't even know you were dating someone."

"Well—I wasn't. But Sam's father came for a visit, and one thing led to another…"

"Oh, how wonderful," Irene sighed. "True love prevails."

"Um. Right." Emma's cheeks went hot. She couldn't tell Irene that love had nothing to do with it, that she'd kept her pregnancy a secret and now they were only getting married for Sam's sake. "Well. I'm leaving for London with him right now. Would you mind helping me pack Sam's things?"

"I'd love to. All his cute, tiny baby things. And now you're off to London, swept away to be wed like a princess in a story." Irene looked wistful. "I hope I find a love like that someday, too."

Her friend's idealistic notion of love, the same dreams she'd once had for herself, cast a pall over Emma's heart. How could she tell Irene that she had nothing to be envious about—that Emma was settling for a loveless marriage so her baby would have a father?

Sam deserves it, she told herself again. She tried to remember the calmness she'd had about her decision just a moment before, when she'd stood in her baby's room, listening to him sleep. She turned away. "I'll be back."

Squaring her shoulders, Emma went down the hall to Alain's office. She took a deep breath and went in.

Her employer was sitting at his desk. He didn't look up. When he spoke, his voice was sour. "Have a good time at the *Tour Eiffel?*"

She was glad he was taking that tone with her.

It made this so much easier. "Yes, I had a wonderful evening," she said sweetly. "Thank you."

Alain glared at her. "I don't appreciate you staying out so late. I was worried."

"I don't appreciate you having me followed."

"I wanted to keep you safe."

"Safe," she said.

"I don't trust Falconeri. You shouldn't, either."

"Right. Well. I'm sorry to tell you, but I have to turn in my notice."

Alain's eyes widened. He slowly rose to his feet. "What?"

"And by *notice,* I mean I'm leaving right now." Her cheeks flamed. "I am actually sorry to do it to you, Alain. It's not very professional. In fact it's completely rude. But Cesare and I are going back to London with the baby…."

"He's stringing you along, Emma, toying with you! I can't believe you would fall for his lines. He'll leave you high and dry when…"

"We're getting married," she said flatly.

Alain's mouth literally fell open.

"What?"

Emma held up her engagement ring, then let her hand drop back to her side. "You've been good to me, Alain. I know you deserve better than me leaving you like this." She swallowed. "But I have to take this chance, for Sam's sake. I'm sorry. I'll never forget your kindness and generosity over the past year...."

"I'm sorry, too," Alain said shortly. "Because you're making a mistake. He ruined Angélique's life."

"Your sister's death was a terrible tragedy, but the coroner ruled the overdose an accident...."

"Accident," he said bitterly. "Falconeri drove my sister to her death. Just as surely as if he'd poured the sleeping pills down her throat."

"You're wrong." Steadying herself, she faced him in his office, clenching her hands at her sides. "He loved her. I know that all too well. He loves her still," she said quietly.

"She gave him everything," Alain continued as if he hadn't heard. "He lured her into marrying him. She loved him. Trusted him." His eyes were wild. "But from the moment they were wed, he neglected her. So much so that she told me she meant to divorce him—then she mysteriously died before she could."

Emma blinked at his implication. "You can't think—"

"If she'd divorced him, he would have gotten nothing. A few hundred thousand dollars. Instead he got her entire fortune. He used that money to turn his shabby little hotel in New York into a multibillion-dollar international hotel conglomerate. You know he's ruthless."

"But not ruthless like that," she whispered. She reminded herself that Alain's words were spoken in anger, that he was a grief-stricken brother. Going toward him, she put her hand gently on his shoulder. "I'm sorry about Angélique. I truly, truly am. But you have to stop blaming Cesare. Her death wasn't his fault. He loved her. He never would have hurt her."

Alain slowly put his hand over her own. "Someday you'll see the man he really is. And you'll come back to me. I'll give you your old job back...or better yet..." His eyes met hers. "I'll give you exactly what Falconeri is offering you now."

Marriage. He meant marriage. Emma swallowed, then pulled her hand away. "I'm sorry, Alain. I care about you deeply, but not in that way." She stepped back from him and said with her heart in her throat, "I wish you all the best. Please take care of yourself." She turned away. "Goodbye."

"Wait."

She turned back at the door. Alain's jaw was tight as he looked at her.

"My sister shone like a star," he said. "She was so beautiful, the life of every party. But even Angélique couldn't keep his attention for long. Don't think you will, either." He faced her across the shadows. "Loving him destroyed her, Emma. Don't let it destroy you."

CHAPTER EIGHT

WHAT A RIDICULOUS warning. Emma still couldn't believe it. It was laughable.

Yes, laughable. Emma felt pleased at the word. She hardly knew which was more ridiculous: the idea that Cesare would have caused his wife, the only woman he'd ever loved, to kill herself with sleeping pills, or that Emma would still be stupid enough to love him, knowing he'd never love her back.

Because she wouldn't.

Love him.

At all.

Ever again.

Even though Cesare had been so wonderful since they'd arrived in London two weeks ago. He'd taken days off from work just to spend time with them, walking across the city, seeing the sights, pushing Sam together in his baby buggy, strolling like all the other happy families along the Thames. But what did Emma care about that?

She certainly wouldn't fall in love with him just because they'd shared champagne while riding the huge Ferris wheel of the London Eye. Or because he'd agreed to a lunch of fish and chips at the Sherlock Holmes pub, when he'd wanted sushi, purely because she'd begged. She didn't care that they'd gone to Trafalgar Square to show Sam the stone lions, and Cesare had taken about a thousand pictures, and let her take some of him making funny faces as he pretended to fall from the stone pedestal. Those memories didn't matter. Her heart was made of stone.

Stone.

They'd visited the National Gallery. The British Museum. They'd gotten a tour of the new Globe Theatre, then bought fresh bread and cheese at the outdoor Borough Market. But her heart was completely safe. Cesare wasn't doing this for her. He was just following through on his promise to be an amazing father to Sam. That was all.

But he was keeping that promise beyond her wildest dreams.

Just yesterday, he'd insisted on going to Hamleys on Regent Street, where he'd bought so many toys that they'd needed to order an extra car to bring all the bags back to the Kensington house.

"When exactly are you expecting Sam to be interested in this?" Emma had asked with a laugh, looking from their sleeping five-month-old baby to the cricket bat and ball on the top of the toy pile.

"He is already fascinated with cricket. Can't you tell?" Cesare had leaned the foam cricket bat across Sam's lap, placing it in the baby's tiny hand as he slept on with a soft baby snore in the stroller. He stepped back. "Look. He's clearly a prodigy."

Holding a foam ball, Cesare elaborately wound his arm, then gently tossed the ball underhand. It bounced off the plastic edge of the stroller and rolled across the floor.

"Prodigy, huh?" she said.

He picked the ball up with a grin. "It might take a bit of practice."

"For him or you?"

"Mostly me. He already seems to have the knack."

"You're just a big kid yourself," she'd teased. "Admit it."

They'd looked at each other, smiling—then the air between them suddenly changed, sizzled with electricity.

Cesare had looked away, muttering something about going to the cashier to pay. And Emma's hands had gripped the stroller handle, as in her mind she repeated the words *In name only* about a thousand times.

Now she shivered as she went up the stairs of the Kensington house. He'd shown her every bit of attention he'd promised, and more. And as promised, he hadn't once tried to kiss her. Not even once.

But that was starting to be a problem. Because in her heart of hearts, she was starting to realize that she wanted him to...

She veered past his bedroom, and continued to her own bedroom, down the hall, where Sam was currently sleeping.

Emma told herself she was being stupid. They weren't even married yet, and she wanted to give him her body? Stupid, stupid. Because how much harder would it be not to give him her heart in the bargain?

We won't be lovers, he'd said in Paris. *We'll be equal partners.*

Her brain had accepted this as the best possible course when she'd agreed to his proposal. And yet...

She was supposed to be planning the wedding right now. But every time she started, something stopped her. Something that had nothing to do with choosing the cake or venue or church.

She was sacrificing her heart. For her son. She could accept that. There was one thing she was trying not to think about.

A marriage in name only would inevitably mean that Cesare would take lovers on the side.

What else could it mean—that Cesare would do as she planned to do, and go without sex for the rest of her life? No. For a red-blooded man like him, that would be impossible.

She was trying not to think about it. Trying and failing.

Emma leaned heavily back against her own bedroom door, closing it behind her. She didn't want to be jealous. She didn't want to be afraid.

But the day they'd returned to Kensington, Emma had fired the housekeeper. Miss Maddie Allen was an attractive young blonde, and Emma had instantly felt she hadn't wanted her within a million miles of Cesare. He'd said he was glad to see her go, that she was the worst housekeeper imaginable and had regularly left iron marks on his shirts. But Emma had given her a year's salary as severance, out of guilt for the real reason she'd fired the beautiful Miss Allen—out of pure, raw fear.

She didn't want to feel this way. With a sigh, Emma walked across her bedroom. A garment bag from a designer shop on Sloane Street was laid carefully upon her bed. Zipping open the bag, she looked down at the gown she would wear tonight at their official engagement party.

For a moment, she just stood there looking at it. Then she reached out and stroked the slinky silver fabric. Pulling off her clothes, she put on a black lace bra and panties and black garter she'd gotten from a French lingerie shop. She didn't dare look at herself in the full-length mirror as she put them on, for fear she'd lose her nerve.

Tonight, she would be introduced to Cesare's

friends, and London society in general, not as his housekeeper, but as his future wife, and the mother of his child. She didn't want to embarrass him.

And if, by some miracle, he thought she looked pretty, maybe their marriage could become real. Maybe he'd take her in his bed, and she'd never have to feel insecure again....

Even Angélique couldn't keep his attention for long. Don't think you will, either.

She pushed away the memory of Alain's words. She had to stop this ugly insecurity! After all her jealousy, she'd found out Cesare hadn't slept with Maddie Allen anyway. Emma knew this because—her blush deepened—she'd blurted out that question immediately after the housekeeper had departed. His reply had been curt.

"No. I did not sleep with her." His jaw had been tight as he looked at the fire in the fireplace, leaving flickering red-and-gold light across the spines of the leatherbound books. He'd parted his lips, drawing in breath as if he meant to say something more, then stopped.

Nearly jumping out of her own skin, she'd said, "But did you ever..."

"No more questions. I won't have you torture us both by asking for a list of my lovers. You of all people know the list is long." Putting his hands on her shoulders, he'd looked down and said softly, "This home is yours now, Emma." He'd cupped her face. "I will never disrespect you here."

His words had thrilled her. *Then.* Later, she'd parsed his words. *This home is yours. I will never disrespect you here.* Meaning—he'd disrespect her elsewhere? At a hotel?

Now, reaching down for the silver dress, long and glamorous like the gown of a 1930s film star, she let the whisper of fabric caress her skin as she pulled it up her body. She didn't want to be jealous. She didn't want to worry.

She wanted him to want—*her.*

Emma's throat tightened. Sitting in the chair at the vanity desk, she began brushing her dark hair with long, hard strokes. She looked at herself in the antique gilt mirror. She was nothing special. Just a regular girl, with round cheeks and big, vulnerable green eyes, who looked scared out of her mind.

How could she marry him, even for Sam's

sake, knowing that Cesare would never uphold the promise of their wedding vows? How could she allow Sam to grow up watching his father repeatedly cheat on his mother—and her explicitly allowing him to do it? What kind of sick ideas would that teach her precious boy about love, marriage, trust and family?

If only Cesare would want her. Her hand slowed with the brush. If only they could truly be lovers, in the same bed, maybe he'd stay true to their wedding vows, and they could be a real family....

"Not ready yet?"

She twisted in the chair to see Cesare in the doorway. He was wearing a tuxedo a little different than the one in Paris—less classic, more cutting edge. But with his dark hair and chiseled good looks, he melted her, whatever he might be wearing. Even wearing nothing.

Especially wearing nothing.

She gulped, turning away. She couldn't stop thinking about the two hot nights he'd made love to her. So long ago now. Almost a year since he'd touched her...

"You look beautiful," he said huskily, coming into her bedroom.

"Oh," she said. "Thank you." Their eyes met in the mirror. Her cheeks turned pink.

"You're just missing one final touch." Coming up behind her, he pulled a sparkling diamond necklace from his pocket and placed it around her neck. Emma's lips parted as she saw it in the mirror, huge diamonds dripping past her collarbone. Involuntarily she put her hand against the necklace, hardly able to believe it was real.

"Almost worthy of the woman wearing it," he murmured.

"You…you shouldn't have." Nervously she rose to her feet, facing him. Realizing her fingertips were still resting against the sparkling stones, she put her hand down.

"It's nothing. A mere trinket." His black eyes caressed her. Leaning forward, he brushed long tendrils of glossy black hair from her bare shoulders, back from the necklace, and whispered, "Nothing is too good for my future wife."

Emma felt the warmth of his breath against her bare skin. She shuddered with a sudden pang of need. Of desire.

She couldn't let herself want him like this. Couldn't. It left her too vulnerable. And the one thing she knew about Cesare was that he detested needy women. She wouldn't, couldn't, be one.

And yet...

Turning away, she went back to the mirror and put on her bright red lipstick with a shaking hand. She tried to ignore his gaze as she ran the red tube carefully over her lips. Sitting back on the bed, she reached for her high-heeled shoes, gorgeous Charlotte Olympia pumps with bamboo on the platform sole and pink cherry blossoms crisscrossing the straps. Emma had seen them in a shop on Sloane Street and in spite of her best efforts—since they were quite expensive—had fallen instantly in love with the 1930s Shanghai glamour.

"Mr. Falconeri said you're to have whatever you wish, madame," the salesgirl had insisted, and Emma, with baby Sam in his stroller next to Cesare's personal bodyguard, had quickly succumbed. It was so wrong to buy shoes that were so expensive. Wrong to want something so forbidden. So clearly out of reach. Emma looked at Cesare.

Or was it?

She rose to her feet, her long black hair tumbling over the low cowl neck of her gown, which melted like liquid silver against her body. She felt transformed—like a glamorous, mysterious starlet from a black-and-white film. She'd never felt so beautiful, or less like the plain, sensible person she'd always been. She took a deep breath, and looked at Cesare.

"I'm ready," she said softly.

He stared at her. She saw his hands tighten at his sides as his gaze slowly went down the length of her dress. And when he spoke, was it her imagination or was his voice a little strained?

"You look…fine." Clearing his throat, he held out his arm. "Ready to meet the firing squad?"

"That's how you refer to your friends?"

He gave her a wicked grin, quirking his dark eyebrow. "You should hear how they refer to me."

"I already know." As she took his arm, Emma's smile fell. "You're the playboy who will never be caught by any woman."

He winked at her, a gesture so silly and unexpected that it caused her heart to twist in her chest. "They'll understand when they meet you."

Their eyes locked, and the squeeze on her heart suddenly became unbearable.

I love you. The words pushed through her soul, through her heart. *I love you, Cesare.*

It was a realization so horrible, Emma sucked in her breath in a gasp so rough and abrupt that it made her double over, coughing.

He rubbed her back, his voice filled with concern. "Are you all right?"

She held up her hand as she regained her breath. Downstairs, she could hear the rising noise of guests arriving at the Kensington mansion for the engagement party. All of his snooty rich friends, and their beautiful girlfriends—half of whom Cesare had probably slept with over the years. Half? Probably more.

"Cara?"

She finally straightened, her eyes watery. "I'm fine," she said, wiping her eyes. It was a lie.

She loved him.

Almost a year ago, she'd left him in despair, believing they had no chance for a future. But now, after just two weeks of wearing his engagement ring on her hand, an awful, desperate hope had pushed itself into her soul. Against her will.

She was in love with him. The truth was she'd never stopped loving him. She was utterly and completely in love with her former boss, the father of her baby.

A man who was going to marry her out of pure *obligation*. Who didn't even want to touch her. Who wanted their marriage to be *in name only*. For their son's sake. A shell. A sham…

"Emma?"

She couldn't let him see her face. Couldn't let him guess what she felt inside. Pretending not to see his outstretched arm, she walked swiftly ahead.

"Wait," he said sharply.

Emma stopped. She took a deep breath, and looked back at him in the hallway.

Smiling down at her in a way that caused his eyes to crinkle, he took her arm and wrapped it around his own. "It's an engagement party. We should enter the ballroom together."

Together. How she wished they could truly be together.

"Are you cold?" He frowned. "You're trembling."

"No… Yes… Um." She twisted her ankle deliberately. "It's the shoes."

He snorted, looking at the four-inch heels. "No wonder."

As they walked down the stairs, she clutched his arm as if her beautiful shoes were really the problem, trying to convince herself everything would be just fine. All right, so she was in love with Cesare and he'd never love her back. All right, so her whole body yearned for him to touch her, but he insisted on separate bedrooms and was likely planning to hook up with the next gorgeous actress who struck his fancy.

But they had a child together. Their marriage would be like a business partnership. That counted for something, didn't it?

Didn't it?

Her throat tightened.

As they approached the mansion's ballroom, she saw his friends—tycoons, actresses, diplomats and royalty. The women were thin and young and beautiful, in chic, tight clothes with no stretch marks from pregnancy. They all turned to look at her speculatively. She could see their sly assumption: that Emma had gotten pregnant on purpose. That was how a gold-digging housekeeper trapped an uncatchable playboy.

Their expressions changed as they looked from her to Cesare. And she realized that being in love with him just made Emma exactly the same as every other woman in the room. They all wanted him. They all broke their hearts over him.

She swallowed, glancing up at him through her lashes, suddenly desperate for reassurance, unable to fight this green demon eating her alive from the inside out.

Cesare abruptly stopped at the bottom of the stairs, in front of the open ballroom doors. "Time to face the music."

His voice was strangely flat. All the emotion had fled from his expression. Meeting her eyes, he gave her a forced smile, as if he already regretted his unbreakable, binding promise to marry her. "Let's get this over with, shall we?"

She suddenly wanted to ask him if those were the words he'd say to himself on their wedding day, too. She looked down at her diamond necklace. At her enormous engagement ring.

I can do this, she told herself. *For Sam.*

Cesare led her into the ballroom, and as she walked across the same marble floor she'd once scrubbed on her hands and knees, she pasted a bright smile on her face as she was formally introduced to London society: the housekeeper who'd been lucky and conniving enough to trap a billionaire playboy into marriage.

"So the great Cesare Falconeri is caught at last," Sheikh Sharif bin Nazih al Aktoum, the emir of Makhtar, said behind him. His voice was amused.

"Caught?" Cesare turned. "I haven't been caught."

The sheikh took a sip of champagne and waved his hand airily. "Ah, but it happens to all of us sooner or later."

Cesare scowled. The two men were not close; he'd invited the sheikh as a courtesy, as his company sought to get permission to build a new resort hotel on one of his Persian Gulf beaches. He'd never thought the man might actually come, but he'd showed up at the Kensington mansion in a black town car with diplomatic flags flying, in full white robes and trailing six bodyguards.

Six. Cesare had to stop himself from rolling his eyes. Bringing two bodyguards was sensible, six was just showing off. He bared a smile at his guest. "I'm the luckiest man on earth to be engaged to Emma. It took me a year to convince her to marry me." Which was true in its way.

The sheikh gave a faint smile. "Some men are just the marrying kind, I suppose."

Cesare raised his eyebrows. "You think *I'm* the marrying kind?"

He shrugged. "Clearly. You've experienced it once and choose willingly to return to it." The dark eyes looked at him curiously, as if Cesare were an exhibit in a zoo. "As for myself, I'm in no rush to be trapped with one woman, subject to her whims, forced to listen to her complain day and night—" He cut himself off with a cough, as if he'd just realized that saying such things at an engagement party might be poor form. "Well. Perhaps marriage is different from the cage I picture it to be."

A cage. Cesare felt the sudden irrational stirrings of buried panic. He could hear the harsh rasp of Angélique's exhausted voice, a decade before.

If you ever loved me, if you ever cared at all, let me go.

But Angélique, you are still my wife. We both gave a promise before God....

Then He will forgive, for He knows how I hate you.

We can go to marriage counseling. He'd reached for her, desperate. *We can get past this.*

Her lip had curled. *What will it take for you to let me go?* She narrowed her eyes maliciously. *Would you like to hear how long and hard Raoul loves me every time we meet, here and in Paris, all this past year, while you've been busy at your pathetic little hotel, trying to make something of yourself? Raoul loves me as you never will.*

Cesare had tried to cover his ears, but she'd told him, until he could bear it no longer and went back on everything he'd ever believed in. *Fine,* he told her grimly. *I'll give you your divorce.*

Twenty-four hours later, Angélique had returned from Buenos Aires and swallowed an entire bottle of pills. Cesare had been the one to find her. He'd found out later that Raoul Menendez was already long married. That he'd laughed in Angélique's face when she'd shown up on his doorstep.

So much for love.

So much for marriage.

Oh, my God. A cold sweat broke out on Cesare's forehead as he remembered that panicked sense of failure and helplessness. The sheikh was right. A cage was exactly what marriage was.

"Your bride is beautiful, of course," the man murmured. "She would tempt any man."

Cesare looked up to see Emma floating by on the dance floor in the arms of Leonidas, his old friend and former wingman at London's best nightclubs. The famous Greek playboy had a reputation even worse than Cesare's. Emma's beautiful face was laughing, lifted to the Greek's admiring eyes. Cesare felt a surge of jealousy.

Emma was his woman. *His.*

"Ah. So lovely. Her long dark hair. Her creamy skin. And that figure..." The sheikh's voice trailed off.

"Don't even think about it," Cesare said dangerously.

He held up his hands with a low laugh. "Of course. I sought merely to praise your taste in a wife. I would not think of attempting to sample her charms myself."

"Good," he growled. "Then I won't have to think of attempting to knock your head off your body."

The man eyed him, then shook his head with a rueful snort. "You have it badly, my friend."

"*It?*"

"You're in love with her."

"She's the mother of my son," Cesare replied sharply, as if that explained everything.

"Naturally," the other man said soothingly. But his black eyes danced, as if to say: *you poor fool, you don't even see how deeply your neck is in the noose.*

Reaching up his hand in an involuntary movement, Cesare loosened the tuxedo tie around his neck. Then he grabbed a glass from a passing waiter and gulped down an entire glass of Dom Perignon in one swallow before he said, "Excuse me."

"Of course."

Going to the other side of the dance floor, Cesare watched Emma dance. He saw the way her face glowed. *Sì.* Think of her. Beautiful. So strong and tender. It wouldn't be so awful, would it, having her in his house?

As long as they didn't get too close.

As long as he didn't try to seduce her.

That was the only way this convenient marriage would ever work. If they kept their distance, so she didn't get any crazy ideas back about loving him. And he didn't start thinking he needed her, or let his walls down.

Vulnerability was weakness.

Love was pain.

Cesare's face went hot as he remembered how he'd felt last year when she'd left him staring after her in the window like a fool. He'd been so sure she'd be back. That she wouldn't be able to resist him.

But she had. Very well.

While he hadn't even slept with another woman since their last night together, almost a year ago.

How the world would laugh if they knew *that* little truth about Cesare Falconeri, the famous playboy. They would laugh—*sì*—they would, because it was pathetic. Fortunately he had no intention of sharing it with anyone. Not even Emma.

He almost had, the first day they'd arrived here, when she'd been so strangely jealous of the silly blonde housekeeper. He'd almost told Emma the truth, but it had caught in his throat. He couldn't let her know that secret. He would never allow himself to be that vulnerable to anyone ever again.

You love her, the sheikh had accused. Cesare snorted. Love? Ridiculous. Love was a concept for idealistic young souls, the ones who thought *lust* was not a big enough word to describe their desire. He'd been that way once. He'd married his wife when he was young and stupid. He'd thought sex meant love. He'd learned his lesson well.

Now his eyes narrowed as he watched Emma smile up encouragingly at Leonidas.

Before he realized what he was doing, he was on the dance floor, breaking up their little duo. "I'd like to dance with my fiancée, if you don't mind."

Emma had been in the middle of laughing but she looked at Cesare in surprise, as if, he thought grimly, she'd already forgotten his existence. As if she already suspected her power over him, and knew his weakness.

Leonidas looked tempted to make some sarcastic remark, but at Cesare's scowl, thought better of it. "Alas, my dear," he sighed to Emma. "I must hand you over to this brute. You belong to him now."

She gave another low laugh, and it was all Cesare could do not to give the Greek shipping tycoon a good kick on the backside to help speed him off the dance floor. With narrowed eyes, he took Emma in his arms.

"Having fun?" he growled as he felt her soft body against his, in her slinky gown of silver.

"It's been dreadful." She peeked up at him. "I'm glad to see you. I know he's your friend, but I didn't think I could take much more. Thank you for saving me!"

"Are you sure?" he said through gritted teeth. "The two of you seemed so cozy."

She blinked. "I was being nice to your friend."

"Not much nicer, I hope," he ground out, "or I might have found the two of you making use of a guest bedroom!"

"What's gotten into you? You're acting almost—"

"Don't say it," he warned.

She tossed her head. "Jealous!"

Cesare set his jaw. "Tell me, what exactly was Leonidas saying that you found so charming?"

Sparks were starting to illuminate her green eyes. "I'm not going to tell you."

He glared at her. "So you admit that you were flirting."

"I admit nothing. You are the one who said we shouldn't ask each other questions!"

"About the past, not the present!"

"That's fine for you, because as you well know, *you* are my only past, while *your* past could fill every bedroom in this mansion. And probably has!"

Her voice caught, and for the first time he heard the ragged edge of repressed tears. He frowned down at her. When he spoke again, his voice was low, barely audible over the music. "What's wrong?"

"Other than you accusing *me* of flirting, while I torture myself with questions every time I meet one of your beautiful guests—wondering which ones you've slept with in the past? And suspecting—all of them!"

Her voice broke. Her green eyes were luminous with unshed tears. He glanced around uneasily at the women around them. Emma was right. He'd slept with more than one of them. No wonder she was upset. He'd nearly exploded with irrational jealousy, just seeing Leonidas talking to her.

Pulling her tighter in his arms, he swayed them to the music, continuing to dance as he spoke to her in a low voice.

"They were one-night stands, Emma. Meaningless."

"You called our first night together *meaningless,* too. The night we conceived our baby."

He flinched. Then emotion surged through him. He glared at her.

"This is why I wanted our marriage to be in name only. To avoid these arguments and stupid jealousies."

"You mean the way you practically hit your good friend in the face for the crime of dancing with me and making me laugh?"

For a moment, he scowled at her. Then, getting hold of himself, he took a deep breath.

"Sorry," he muttered. "I never meant…to make you cry."

Emma looked away, blinking fast. "That's not why I was crying."

"What is it, then?"

"It's stupid."

"Tell me."

She swallowed.

"They all think I'm a sly gold digger. All your friends." She wiped her eyes. "A few women actually *congratulated* me on tricking you into marriage. Some of them could hardly believe a woman as—well, fat—as me could do it. Others just wanted tips for how to trick billionaire husbands of their own. They wanted to know if I poked holes in the condom wrapper with a needle or what."

Cesare's hands tightened on her back. He stared down at her, vibrating with rage as they swayed to the music. "I will take a horsewhip to all of them."

She gave a small laugh, even as tears spilled down her cheeks. "It doesn't matter," she said softly, but he could feel how much that wasn't true. To her, the simple question of honor and a good name did matter. Her pride had been hurt.

He fiercely wiped a tear off her cheek with her thumb. "You and I, we know the truth."

"Yes. We do. But I still wish," she whispered, "we were a million miles from here."

"From London?"

"As long as we're in London, I'll always be your gold-digging housekeeper. And you'll be the playboy who's slept with every woman in the city." She looked up at him with tearful eyes. "I wish we could just go. Move away. Somewhere I'll never have to wonder, every time I see another woman, if she's ever been in your bed." She shuddered. "I hate what my imagination is doing to me—"

"Since the first night we slept together, I haven't touched another woman."

Her lips parted. "What?"

Cesare was almost as surprised as she was that he'd said it. But damn it—how could he not tell her? He couldn't see her pain and do nothing. "It's true."

"But—why?"

He stopped on the dance floor.

"I haven't wanted to," he said quietly.

"I don't understand." Emma shook her head. "If that's the case, why would you say you wanted a marriage in name only?"

Reaching out, he brushed back some dark hair from the soft skin of her bare shoulder above her gown. "Because all my love affairs have ended badly."

She swallowed. "Mine, too."

"Our marriage is too important. I cannot let it end in fights and tears and recriminations. The only way to make sure our relationship never ends…is never to start it in the first place."

"It won't work. Listen to us! We're still fighting anyway."

"Not like we would if—" He cut himself off, then shook his head. "You know lovers are a dime a dozen to me. But you… You are special." Reaching up, he stroked her cheek. "I need you as a partner. As my friend." He set his jaw. "Sex would ruin everything. It always does."

Swallowing, she exhaled, looking away.

"All right," she said finally. "Friends." There was a shadow of worry behind her eyes as they lifted to his. "You really haven't slept with any other women?" she said in wonder. "Since the night we conceived Sam?"

He gave her an unsteady grin. "Don't tell anyone. It would ruin my reputation."

"Your secret is safe with me." She smiled up at him, even as her eyes still shone with tears. "And you might as well know—your friend Leonidas is a very clumsy dancer. That's why I was laughing at his dumb jokes. To try to disguise yelps of pain every time he stomped on my foot."

A hard pressure in Cesare's chest suddenly released. For a moment, they just looked at each other, and though they were in the middle of a dance floor surrounded by a hundred guests, it was as if it were just the two of them in the world.

He never should have brought her back to London, Cesare thought suddenly. Of course not. How could he have expected Emma to return as a wife to the house where she'd once been his employee, and sleep in the same lonely bedroom down the hall from the bed where he'd seduced other women, again and again? The house where he'd once expected her, as a matter of course, to make breakfast for his one-night-stands and escort them out with gifts and a shoulder to cry on?

"We don't have to stay here," he said slowly. "There's someplace else we can go. A place where we can be married and start fresh, just the three of us. As a family."

"Where?"

His heart twisted to remember it. But he forced himself to meet her gaze. To smile.

"Home," he said simply.

CHAPTER NINE

THE TWO-HUNDRED-year-old villa on the shores of Lake Como stood like an ancient castle, caught in the shadows between the gray water and lowering clouds of dusk.

Emma took a deep breath, savoring the cool air against her cheeks and crunch of gravel beneath her feet as she walked along the forest path around the lake toward home. From the cushioned front pack on her chest, Sam let out another low cry, waving his plump arms. She sighed, looking down at her baby, then rubbed his soft downy hair.

"I thought for sure that a walk would do it," she said mournfully. He was irritable because he hadn't gone down for a nap all day, not for lack of her trying. "Ah, well. Let's see what we can rustle up for dinner, shall we?"

Her own stomach was growling after their long walk. She had spent hours trying to coax him to sleep, but as tired as Sam was, as soon as he started to nod off, he kept jerking himself awake. Now, she was finally forced to admit failure. The darkening October sky was drawing her back home.

That, and knowing Cesare was waiting for them...

Emma smiled to herself as she walked the lake path back toward the villa, which had been in the Falconeri family for hundreds of years. They'd been living here a month now, and it was starting to feel like home, though their first day, when he'd shown her around, she'd been shocked. "You grew up in this palace?" she'd blurted out, thinking of her two-bedroom bungalow on the Texas prairie.

He'd snorted. "It didn't always look like this. When I was a child, we barely had indoor plumbing. Our family ran out of money long before I was born. And that was even before my parents decided to devote their lives to art." His lips quirked. "Five years ago, I decided I wouldn't let it fall apart." His voice turned grim. "Although I was tempted."

"I remember you talking about the remodel."

Emma had walked through room after room, all of them with ceilings fifteen feet high, with gilded details on the walls and even a fresco in the foyer. "I never imagined I might someday live here as your wife."

She could see why the remodel of this house, which she remembered him grumbling about, had required so much money and time. Every detail of the past had been preserved, while made modern with brand-new fixtures, windows, heated floors and two separate kitchens.

She'd been amazed when she saw a beautiful oil painting of Cesare as a young boy of maybe three or four, with chubby cheeks and bright innocence in his eyes—along with a determined set to his jaw. His clothes were ragged and covered with mud. She'd pointed at it with a laugh. "That was you?"

"My mother painted me perfectly. I was always outside in the garden, growing something or other."

"You liked to garden?" It astonished Emma. She couldn't reconcile the image of the happy, grimy boy in the painting with the sophisticated tycoon who now stood before her.

He rolled his eyes. "We were that kind of family. If I wanted fruit, I had to grow it myself. My parents' idea of childcare was to give me a stick and send me outside to play in the dirt." He fell silent. "But for all that, we were happy. We loved each other."

"I'm sorry," she'd whispered, seeing the pain in his eyes. She'd put her arms around him. "But we're here now."

For a moment, Cesare had allowed her to hold him, to offer comfort. Then he'd pulled away. "It all worked out," he said gruffly. "If I hadn't had my little tragedy and been sent to New York, I might never have started Falconeri International." His lips curved. "Who knows. I might still have been living here in a ruin, growing oranges and flowers, digging in the garden."

Now, as Emma walked along the lake's edge with her baby in her front pack, she stared at that overgrown garden. Alone of everything on the estate, the villa's garden had not been touched. It had been left untended and wild, choked with weeds. It was as if, she thought, Cesare could neither bear to have it destroyed, nor have it returned to its former glory.

A white mist was settling across the lake, thick and wet. Emma shivered as she pushed open the tall, heavy oak door that led into the Villa Falco-neri. The scrape of the door echoed against the checkered marble floor and high ceiling with its two-hundred-year-old fresco above, showing pastoral scenes of the countryside.

"Cesare?" she called.

There was no answer. Emma heard a soft snore from her front pack and looked down. After hours of trying, Sam had finally dropped to sleep. His dark eyelashes fluttered downward over his plump cheeks. Smiling to herself, she went upstairs to tuck him into his crib.

She was sharing her beautiful bedroom with her baby. There was plenty of room for his crib and changing table. The room was enormous, in powder-blue, with a canopy bed and a huge window with a balcony overlooking the lake. Gently lifting her sleeping baby out of the carrier, she tucked him into his bed.

Alone in the room, without her baby's warmth against her, she felt a shiver of cold air in the deepening twilight. Even here, in this beautiful place, she slept alone.

You are special. I need you as a partner. As my friend. Sex would ruin everything.

Emma took a deep breath.

Tomorrow, their three-day wedding celebration would begin, first with a church ceremony, followed by a civil service the next day. Private celebrations with just a few friends: a white dress. A cake. Vows that could not be unspoken.

How she wished it all could be real. She longed to be his real wife. She looked at her empty bed. She wanted to sleep in his arms, to feel his lips on hers, to feel his hard, naked body cover hers at night. A flash of heat went through her and she touched her lips with her fingers. She could remember him there…

She shivered, closing her eyes.

As much as her brain told her that marriage was the rational solution, as much as her heart longed to be permanently bound to the man she loved, her body was tense and fighting the wedding every step of the way.

Marry a man who would never touch her?

A man who was still in love with his long-dead wife?

A man who would satisfy his sexual needs elsewhere, discreetly, leaving Emma to grow old and gray and die in a lonely, solitary bed?

Emma had been shocked when Cesare had told her in London that he hadn't slept with another woman since their first night together. But as amazing as that was, she knew it wouldn't last. It couldn't. Cesare wasn't the kind of man to tolerate an empty bed for the rest of his life. There were too many women in the world who would eagerly join him, married or no.

Cesare didn't equate sex with love the way she did, either. To Cesare, satisfying a sexual need was no different than satiating a hunger for food or sleep. It was just physical. Not emotional.

Lovers are a dime a dozen to me.

Emma swallowed, crossing her arms over her body.

She could ask him outright if he planned to be unfaithful to her. But she was afraid, because if she asked, he would tell her the truth. And she didn't think her heart could take it.

No, it was easier to live in denial, in the pretty lie of marriage vows, and to try not to think about the ugly truth beneath....

"There you are, *cara*."

Whirling around to see Cesare in the doorway, she put a finger to her lips. "Shh. Sam is finally asleep," she whispered, barely loud enough to hear. "I just got him down."

His handsome face looked relieved. *"Grazie a dio."* He silently backed away, and she followed him out of the room. She closed the door behind them, and they both exhaled.

"What made him sleep? Was it your walk?"

"No," she said softly. "I think it was coming home."

For a long moment, they looked at each other.

"I'm glad you are thinking of it as home, *cara.*" He smiled. "And starting tomorrow, we will be husband and wife."

A lump rose in her throat. She tried to stay silent, but her fear came out in blurted words. "Are you still sure it's what you want?"

The smile slid from his face. "Why wouldn't I be?"

"A lifetime without love—without…" She gulped, then forced herself to meet his gaze. "Without sex…"

"The decision has already been made." His voice had turned cold. "I've made you dinner. Come."

She was very hungry after her walk, but she hesitated, glancing behind her. "I can't just leave Sam up here. Not until the baby monitor arrives. This house is so big and the old walls are thick. Downstairs in the dining room, we'd never hear him if he cried...."

"I thought you might feel that way." Cesare tilted his head, looking suddenly pleased with himself. "We're not going far."

Placing his hand in the small of her back, he pushed her gently down the hall. A sizzle of electricity went up her body at even that courteous, commanding touch. Biting her lip, she allowed him to lead her...

...a mere ten steps, to his own bedroom next door.

"We're having dinner in your room?" she said, a little sheepish that he'd guessed her feelings about the baby so well.

He nodded. "A private dinner for two on my balcony."

"Lovely," she said. "Um...any particular reason?"

"I just thought before our guests arrive in the

morning, it would be nice to have a quiet dinner. To talk."

"Oh." That sounded ominous. The last time they'd had a private dinner and a talk she'd walked out engaged, with her whole life changed forever. She was afraid what might come out of it this time. The questions she might ask. The answers he might give. All words that could never be unheard or forgotten.

She licked her lips and tried to smile as she repeated, "Lovely."

Cesare led her into his enormous en suite bedroom, with a fireplace and a huge bed that she tried not to look at as they walked past it. He led her out to the balcony, where she found a charming table for two, lit by candlelight, and two silver plates covered by lids. Beyond the table, the dark sweep of Lake Como trailed moonlight in a pattern of gold.

Emma looked at Cesare, noticing for the first time how he had carefully dressed in a crisp black shirt and pants. With his dark hair, black eyes and chiseled jawline, he looked devastatingly handsome. He was the man every woman wanted. While she... Well.

Emma touched her hair, which was tumbling over her shoulders, messy from Sam tugging on it, and from the wind of their walk. She looked down at her simple pink blouse and slim-fit jeans. "I'm not dressed for this." For all she knew, she might have baby spit-up on her shoulder. She tried to look, but she couldn't see. "Um. I should go change…"

"Go back to your bedroom and risk waking up our son? Don't you dare. Besides." He looked over her body with a heavily lidded gaze. "You are perfect just as you are." He held out her chair with a sensual smile. *"Signorina, per favore."*

Nervously Emma sat down. He sat down across from her, poured them each a glass of wine, then lifted off the silver lids of the plates. She took a deep breath of fettuccine primavera, with breaded chicken, salad and fresh bread. Placing the linen napkin in her lap, she picked up her heavy fork, also made of solid silver. "This looks delicious."

"It is an old family recipe."

"You cooked it yourself?"

"Not the bread, but the pasta, yes. I had to do something to be useful while you were fighting the war to put Sam to sleep." He paused. "I had

Maria pick up the vegetables from town, but I made the sauce as well."

"I had no idea you knew how to cook."

He gave a low laugh. "When I was a boy, I helped with everything. Milked our cow. Made cheese and grew vegetables in the garden."

"Your life is very different now." She sipped red wine. She wasn't going to ask him if he planned to be faithful after their marriage. She *wasn't*. Placing a trembling hand over her throat to keep the question from popping out, she asked in a strained tone, "So why have you let the garden grow so wild and unloved? I could cut back the weeds, and bring it back to its former glory...."

His hand tightened on his wineglass, even as he said politely, "It's not necessary."

"I wouldn't mind. After all, it's my home, too, now...."

The candlelight flickered in the soft, invisible breeze. "No."

His short, cold word echoed across the table. As their eyes locked, Emma's heart cried out. For all the things they both weren't saying.

Was this to be their marriage? Courtesy, without connection? Proximity without words?

Would this beautiful villa become, like the Kensington mansion had been, her empty, lonely tomb?

Taking another gulp of wine, she blinked fast, looking out at the dark, quiet night. Lights of distant villas sparkled like stars across the lake. She heard the cry of unseen night birds, and the soft sigh of wind rattling the trees.

"How did you first meet her?" she asked softly. "Your wife?"

"Why do you want to know?" He sounded guarded.

"I'm going to be your wife tomorrow. Is it so strange that I'd want to hear the story of the first Mrs. Falconeri? Unless—" she bit her lip and faltered "—you still can't bear to speak of her…"

For a moment, she thought he wasn't going to answer. Then he exhaled. "I was twenty-three." He paused. "I'd inherited my uncle's hotel. Not the hotel you worked at on Park Avenue, but an old, rickety fleabag on Mulberry Street. I struggled to keep it afloat, working each day until I dropped, doing everything from carrying luggage to bookkeeping to making breakfast." He paused. "Angélique stumbled into the lobby one evening, taking cover from a rainstorm."

He fell silent. He cut a piece of chicken, took a bite. Set his fork and knife down. Emma leaned forward over the table, on edge for what he would say next, barely aware of the cool night breeze against her overheated skin.

Cesare looked out at the dark, moonswept lake, haunted with October mist. "For me," he said softly, "it was love at first sight."

Emma's heart lurched in her chest.

"She was so glamorous, ten years older, sexually experienced and—well, French..."

Everything she was not. Emma felt the pain twist more deeply beneath her ribs.

"We were married just six weeks after we met."

"That's fast," Emma mumbled. He'd known her for almost eight *years*.

"I was dazzled by her. It seemed like a miracle that she wanted to marry me. After we wed, I was more determined than ever to make the hotel a success. No one would ever accuse me of living off my wife."

"No," she whispered over the lump in her

throat. She took another gulp of wine, finishing off her glass.

"She was unique," Cesare said in a low voice. "My first."

He couldn't mean what she thought he meant. "Your—first?"

"Yes," he said quietly.

"But—you were *twenty-three.*"

"Amusing, yes?" His lips curved. "The famous playboy, a virgin at twenty-three. My uncle was strict, and after he died, I was too focused on the hotel. I had no money, nothing to offer any potential wife."

It was a good thing she hadn't been drinking wine or she would have spit it out in shock. "You were trying to save yourself—for marriage?"

"I was idealistic," he said quietly. "I thought love was supposed to be part of it." He glanced behind him at the villa, then at the dark water, scattered with gold and silver moonlight like diamonds on citrine. "Then it all died."

Yes. She'd died. His one and only love.

"You still love her, don't you?" Emma choked out. "And you always will."

Cesare's dark eyes abruptly focused on her. He

put his hands over hers and said softly, "It doesn't matter."

She felt the warmth of his hands over hers, beneath the dizzying stars in the wide black-and-violet sky. Her heart beat frantically in her chest. She wanted to throw herself at his feet. To beg him to be faithful. To beg him to forget his long-dead wife and love her, instead.

"Of course it matters," she said hoarsely. "My father used to say love is all that matters. It's the only thing we leave behind."

His expression hardened. "We both love Sam."

"But is that truly enough for you to be happy?"

"Marriage isn't about happiness," he said. "It's about keeping a promise. Until death do us part. And the truth is, you and I are already bound together. By our child."

Bound, Emma thought unhappily. Bound like a rope around his wrists. Like a shackle. Like a chain.

She rose unsteadily to her feet. "I can't do this."

"What?"

"Marry you." She shook her head tearfully. "I can't let this beautiful villa be turned into a tomb, like your house was for me in Kensington, with nothing but silence and shadows to fill my bed.... I can't spend the rest of my life alone. Trapped with a man who doesn't even want me."

"You think I don't want you?" His voice was dangerous.

"You say that I am special," she said bitterly. "Your partner. Your *friend.* But we both know, once we are wed, you'll take lovers. But I won't. Because—I..." *I love you,* she almost said, but her throat closed when she saw Cesare's face.

"Not *want* you. My God." There was fury in his black eyes as he stood in the moonlight. "I told you I haven't touched another woman in over a year, and you think I don't want you?"

Her mouth suddenly went dry. "You—"

"You have no idea how hard it's been not to touch you." Reaching out, he slowly stroked down her neck, then leaned forward and whispered, "I've yearned to have you in my bed. Every night. I've thought of nothing else—but you."

Sparks flew up and down her body everywhere he touched.

"But I was trying to do the right thing for once in my damned life," he ground out. "In sickness and in health. For richer or for poorer. I was trying to do the right thing for our son. But the truth is all I've been able to think about, every single night, is having you naked beneath me."

Emma couldn't breathe.

Cesare's gaze dropped to her lips. "And this is my reward for my sacrifice. You mean nothing more to me now than the housekeeper you were. You think—"

His voice ended with a growl as he ripped her into his arms. Holding her against his chest in the moonlight, he lowered his head, then stopped, his mouth an inch from hers.

Emma trembled at the warmth of his breath. She could almost taste his lips. Electricity seared through her veins.

"Please," she whispered, hardly knowing what she was asking for. She licked her lips, felt her tongue almost brush against his skin. She shuddered with blinding need, from her body to her heart. *He doesn't love me. His heart is buried with his wife.* "Lust," she breathed aloud, staring at his lips. "It's just lust."

She heard his harsh intake of breath. In sudden movement, he pushed her against the wall, and lowered his mouth to hers in a savage, hungry kiss.

Sparks sizzled down her skin as she felt his body, hard against hers. His hand roamed down her neck, ruthlessly reaching beneath the neckline of her blouse, to cup her breast beneath her bra. She gasped as she felt his hand brush her aching nipple. As her lips parted in the gasp, he deepened the kiss, twining and flicking his tongue against hers. He took her mouth roughly, in a way that left no doubt who was master.

A soft moan came unbidden from deep inside her. Her arms rose of their own accord to wrap around his shoulders. His tall, muscular body pressed against hers, hip to hip, and she felt lost in his passionate embrace. She clutched his back, feeling the steel of his muscles beneath his shirt. His hips swayed, grinding against her.

Cesare kissed her, his tongue twisting hot and hard in her mouth, tangling, giving and taking. And Emma knew that whatever her brain told her she should want, that in her body and heart she'd wanted this, only this, for the past year. For years before that.

The truth was that she'd waited for it all her life.

But this wasn't just lust for her. No matter how she'd tried to convince him otherwise. The truth was trembling inside her. *I love you. I never stopped loving you.*

Her hands reached up, tangling in his short black hair. She pulled him closer, clutching his shoulders, lifting on her tiptoes to kiss him with all the anguished love in her heart. He gripped her hard against the rough stone wall.

They kissed on the balcony, with the moon-swept lake at their feet, and if a cool October wind blew against Emma's overheated skin, she no longer felt it. Cesare's hands moved over her body, sliding down her thin blouse, up her arms. Her breasts were crushed against his hard chest, and every inch of her was on fire.

His kiss possessed her with an intensity and force she'd never felt before. It was as if she alone could save him from destruction, as if he were taking her very breath to live.

When he drew back, he looked down at her, his eyes wide. Tilting back her head, he gently ran his thumbs over her full, swollen lips.

"Tell me to stop," he said with a shuddering breath. "For God's sake. Tell me now…"

But she couldn't. She could no more tell him to stop than she could tell herself to stop breathing, or the stars to stop shining. She loved him, and for one more night, the pathetic truth was that she was willing to do anything, pay any price.

With a low groan, he lifted her up into his arms as if she weighed nothing at all and carried her through the balcony door into his bedroom. He set her down gently on the enormous bed.

Still dressed, he covered her body with his own, pressing her back against the softness of the white pillows and thick white comforter as he kissed her. She felt the roughness of his chin against her skin, felt the heat and strength of his body. His hands trailed down her throat, to the hollow of her collarbone, then along the sides of her body, over her blouse. Her breasts felt full and heavy, her nipples tight.

She felt him unbuttoning her blouse. Never breaking their kiss, he slowly pulled it off her body, in a whisper of fabric skimming against her skin. Her hands trembled as she did the same with his black shirt, overwhelmed with desire to feel his heat. Her fingertips ran down the muscles of his back, and she tossed his shirt to the floor.

Looking up at him in the moonlight, she saw the stark shadows beneath the lines of his hard chest, the trail of dark hair down his taut belly. Her fingers traced down his velvety-smooth skin, over the powerful muscles of his body.

With a low growl, he kissed and stroked down her skin, nibbling her chin, down her neck to the valley between her breasts. Undoing the front clasp of the bra with a well-practiced movement, he cupped her full breasts with his large hands. She shivered at the sensation, but he continued down her body, flicking his tongue in her belly button, grasping her hips. Unbuttoning her jeans, he slowly pulled them down her legs, along with her panties, before tossing them to the floor.

She felt his shoulders between her bare legs, the heat of his breath on the sensitive, tender skin between her thighs. She gripped his shoulders in agonizing anticipation, then felt his tongue slide between her legs to her deepest, most secret place. He brushed his tongue against her, pushing two fingertips inside her—slowly, so slowly—until her body was so tight that she gripped his shoulders, holding her breath.

"Wait…" she gasped.

He refused to obey. He ruthlessly pushed her to the limit, and beyond, until with a soft scream she exploded beneath the unrelenting pleasure of his tongue between her legs. The moment she cried out, gripping her fingernails into his flesh, he ripped off the rest of his clothes. He shoved himself roughly inside her, ramming to the hilt in a single deep thrust.

The sensation of him filling her, just seconds after her ecstasy, caused a shocking new wave of pleasure to build inside her. He thrust again, and she gasped with the sensation of a new wave of desire, taking off from the level it had been a moment before, climbing higher and higher, tighter and tighter. She began to rock back and forth, trembling with almost unbearable pleasure.

He rode her harder, faster, panting for breath, as their sweaty bodies clung together in the dark, hot night. A cool breeze whipped in from the Italian lake, banging back the balcony doors. But neither of them noticed as he was deep, pounding inside her, splitting her apart. She gasped, clutching his taut backside, feeling his muscles grow hard as stone beneath her hands. With a shuddering intake of breath, he slammed inside her one last time, and they both let go, flying, falling, collapsing into thin air.

Cesare landed on top of her, then, as if he feared he would hurt her with his weight, immediately rolled on one side of her. He pulled her against him on the bed, nuzzling her forehead, both of them so close, so close. Both of them the same.

Emma closed her eyes. She suddenly felt like weeping.

A moment before, all she'd wanted was this, only this. But now, she'd barely had what she wanted and already wanted more. Not just sex. She was greedy beyond all imagining. She wanted his love.

In this moment of glory, heartache filled her. She pulled away from him, moving into the shadows of the bed.

"What is it, *cara?*" he asked in a low voice, as his hand gently stroked her bare back. She knew she shouldn't answer. She should just leave it.

But the words came out of her throat against her will.

"Will you be faithful to me?" she whispered. "Can you be?"

For a moment, he didn't answer. She couldn't

see his face. And she knew she'd made a horrible mistake. She turned to face him on the bed.

"Is fidelity so important to you?" he said in a low voice.

The lump in her throat suddenly felt like a razorblade.

"No," she whispered. Really, what use was fidelity without love? What was it but cold pretense, the form of love without the heart of it?

"Tomorrow we wed." Sleepily he pulled her into his arms and kissed her forehead. "So many nights I dreamed of you, *cara,* did you know that? And now you are in my bed. Our wedding night before we are wed…"

"Yes." She ran her fingertips along the warmth of his bare chest. She would marry him tomorrow. She'd given her word. She would raise his child and sleep in his bed, and be at his command for the rest of her life. And Cesare, the onetime playboy who notoriously enjoyed such a variety of women, would do his best to accomplish his obligation of fidelity—at least for a month, or possibly a year…

Holding her in his arms, he closed his eyes. A

few moments later, his breathing became even and deep.

But Emma didn't have the same peace.

She leaned against his naked body, so warm and powerful and protective around her own. She looked through the open balcony door, past the moonlight to the distant bright star, the first star of morning. In a few hours, the dark violet sky would change to red, then pink, then a glorious Italian blue as the sun would rise on her wedding day. The first and only wedding day she'd ever know. She'd be married to the man she loved. The father of her baby.

Cesare would marry her. For Sam's sake.

But what happiness could they know, in a marriage where only one partner loved, and was faithful?

The truth was that, wedding or not, Emma was no better than any of the other women Cesare might take to his bed.

His real wife was, and always would be, Angélique.

Loving him destroyed her, Emma. Don't let it destroy you.

Emma shuddered this time as she remembered

Alain's words. He knew how wildly his sister had loved Cesare. What he hadn't known was the fierce love Cesare had for her in return. Angélique hadn't been destroyed by loving him.

But Emma would be.

She looked at Cesare's handsome sleeping face in the shadowy bedroom. She listened to the sound of his breath. Could she really marry him? Knowing she'd be nothing more than the mother of his child, the keeper of his home, or at best—a warm body in the night?

Could Emma accept an eternity of knowing she was the other woman—that if given the choice, her husband would have traded her life in an instant for Angélique's?

You're stronger than you know, kiddo. She heard her father's words. *You'll get through this, and have a life more amazing than you can even imagine. Filled with sunshine and flowers and above all, love. All the things you deserve, Emma. I love you, sweetheart.*

Blinking fast, Emma stared out at the dark lake. The last streak of silvery moonlight stretched out before her like a path, like a single forlorn tear, leading to an unseen future.

* * *

Cesare held her hand tightly, unable to look away from her beautiful face.

Emma was wearing a beautiful wedding dress, holding a bouquet of pink roses. But somehow, as they left the chapel, her fingers slipped from his grasp. She ran ahead of him. He called her name, and she glanced back, laughing as she disappeared in the mist. He saw her plummet down the chapel steps, down, down, down, her bouquet exploding into a million pale pink petals falling thickly like snow.

His feet were heavy as concrete as he tried to reach her. It seemed an eternity before he found her, on a soft bed of grass. But something had changed. Emma's beautiful face had turned hollow-cheeked like his mother's, her eyes blank with despair like Angélique's. Emma was dying, and he knew it was his fault. Desperate, he jumped on a boat and took off across the lake to find a doctor. But halfway across, the boat's engine died, leaving him stranded and alone, surrounded by dark water, and he suddenly knew he was too late to save her. He looked down at water like black glass in the moonlight. There was only one thing to do now…only one way to end the pain…

With a shuddering gasp, Cesare sat up straight in bed.

Still panting for breath, he looked out the window. The sky was blue. The sun was shining. He heard birds singing. It was a dream, he told himself. All a dream. But his body was covered with cold sweat.

Today was his wedding day.

He looked down at the bed where he'd made love to her last night. Empty. He put out his hand. The sheets were long cold.

Cesare suddenly wondered if he might have woken her with his nightmare, tossing and turning or worse, crying out. He clawed back his hair, exhaling with a flare of nostril. The thought of being so vulnerable was horrifying.

But not as much as what he was about to do today.

Naked, he got up from the bed, and his legs seemed to shake beneath him. Downstairs, he could already hear guests arriving. Some twenty people, friends and acquaintances from London, Rome and around the world, would be staying at the villa for the next three days. Today, there would be a long prewedding lunch, followed by a ceremonial church wedding at twilight in the small, ancient chapel on his estate. Tomorrow they'd have the civil service in town.

The next three days would be nothing but one party after another, and the thought suddenly made him grit his teeth. He'd chosen this. Shouldn't he feel satisfaction, or failing that, at least some kind of resigned peace?

Instead his body shook with a single primal emotion—fear.

I can do it for Sam.

Closing his eyes, he pictured his sweet baby's face. Then the woman holding his son in her arms.

Emma. Her beauty. Her kindness. She was the perfect mother to Sam. The perfect homemaker. The perfect lover. He thought of the ecstasy he'd experienced last night in her arms. But reflecting on all the ways he valued Emma didn't calm the frantic beat of his heart. To the contrary. It just made him feel more panicked.

He'd sworn he'd never have a child. Then he'd found out about Sam.

He'd sworn he'd never marry again. Then he'd proposed to Emma.

He'd sworn their marriage would be in name only. Then he'd swept her straight into bed last night.

What was next? What fresh vow would he break?

There was only one left, and it was a line that he could not, would not cross. Because if he did, if he ever let himself love her, he'd be utterly annihilated. Just like before…

With an intake of breath, he paced across the bedroom, the same grand room which, decades before, had belonged to his parents. So in love, before everything came crashing down.

Whether by death, or divorce, love always ended. And ended in pain.

Cesare couldn't let himself love Emma. It would be the final bomb exploding his life into pieces. Any time he tried to love someone, to depend on them, they left—as far and fast as they possibly could. Through death.

He couldn't survive it again.

His heart pounded frantically. He looked out the window, past the overgrown garden, toward the lake. He should never have brought Emma here. Never should have let himself see the bright laughter in her eyes as she held their baby yesterday, carrying him through that garden. *This is a lemon tree, and this is verbena...*

Just as his own mother had once done. He could still remember his mother's warm embrace, back when he was very young and happy and thought the sunshine would last forever. He could hear his father's deep, tender voice. *Ti amo, tesoro mio.*

Cesare shuddered, blinking fast. He'd thought if he was careful not to love anyone, never to care, that he would be safe. Instead he'd accidentally created a child.

Or had it been an accident? Some part of him must have been willing to take that risk—since he'd never slept with any woman without protection before. Not even Angélique. But then, she'd been too selfish to want a child. All she'd wanted was a man to worship her, and when Cesare had gotten too busy with work, she'd found another man to offer her the worship she desperately craved.

Emma was nothing like Angélique. If the Frenchwoman had been cold and mysterious as moonlight, Emma was sunlight on a summer's day. Warmth. Life.

But he couldn't let himself love her. She could leave him. She could die. Her cancer could return, and leave Cesare, like his father, bereft at midnight on an endless black lake.

Looking out at Lake Como, he had the sudden impulse to throw on his clothes and run away from this house. From this wedding. Far, far away, where grief and pain and need could never find him again.

Stop it. Cesare took a deep breath, clenching his hands at his sides. *Get ahold of yourself.* He couldn't fall to pieces. He had to marry her. He'd promised. His child deserved a real home, like he'd once had. Before his parents had abruptly left, stripping his happiness away without warning...

Closing his eyes, he took a deep breath. He ruthlessly forced down his feelings. Shut down his heart.

Jaw tight, he opened his eyes. He would marry Emma today. Whatever he felt now, he'd given his word. He would marry her and never, ever love her.

And no irrational nightmare, no mere *terror*, would stop him from fulfilling his promise.

CHAPTER TEN

"OH, EMMA," IRENE whispered. Her eyes sparkled with tears. "You make such a beautiful bride."

Looking at herself in the gilded full-length mirror, Emma hardly recognized herself. The sensible housekeeper had been magically transformed into a princess bride from a nineteenth-century portrait. Her beautiful cream-colored silk dress had been handmade in Milan, with long sleeves and elaborate beadwork. Her black hair was pulled up in a chignon, tucked beneath a long veil that stretched all the way to the floor.

The green eyes looking back at her in the mirror were the only thing that seemed out of place. They weren't tranquil. They were tortured.

Just last night, passion had curled her toes and made her cry out with pleasure. That morning, she'd risen from the warmth of their bed early to feed Sam. She had drowsed off while rocking the baby back to sleep, and when she returned later, Cesare was gone.

But something had changed in him. All day, as they welcomed their newly arriving guests—who, with the exception of Irene, were all Cesare's friends, not hers—he'd barely looked at her. She'd told herself he was just busy, trying to be a good host. But the truth was that in the tiny corner of her heart, she feared it was more than that. No. She *knew* it was more than that.

This marriage was a mistake.

Emma looked at herself again in the mirror, at the beautiful wedding gown. She smoothed the creamy silk beneath her hands. *The decision is already made,* she told herself, but her hands were trembling.

Since she'd left his bed that morning, the day had flown by, in a succession of celebrations leading up to tonight's first wedding ceremony, at twilight in the chapel. Emma had been genuinely thrilled to see Irene, who'd been flown in from Paris courtesy of Cesare. But as she'd shown the younger woman around her new home, Irene's idealistic joy had soon become grating.

"It's all like a dream," she'd breathed, seeing

her beautifully appointed guest room, with its Louis XV furniture and accents of deep rose and pale pink. She'd whirled to face Emma, her rosy face shining. "You deserve this. You worked so hard, you put your baby first, and now you've been rewarded with a wedding to a man who loves you with all his heart. It's just like a fairy tale."

Feeling like a fraud, Emma had muttered some reply, she couldn't even remember what. Later, as she was congratulated by his friends, even a sheikh of some sort with long white robes who, in perfect British English, wished her well, the feeling only worsened.

Out of everyone at the villa, only one person didn't speak to her. He didn't even look at her. Not since he'd made love to her last night.

How could he turn so fast from passion to coldness?

The answer was clear.

Cesare didn't want to marry her.

It was only his promise that was forcing him to do it. Emma's gaze fell on baby Sam, who was currently lying on her soft bed, proudly chewing the tip of his own sock, which was stretched out from his foot.

"Here's your bouquet," Irene said now, smiling as she wiped her own happy tears away. She handed her a small, simple bouquet of small red roses. "Perfect. This is all so romantic.…"

Emma looked down at the flowers, feeling cold. How could she destroy Irene's dreams, and tell her that *romantic* was the last thing this wedding would be? She exhaled.

"I just wish my father were here," Emma whispered. With his steady hand and good advice, he'd know just what to do.

Irene's face instantly sobered. "It must be so hard not to have him here, to walk you down the aisle. But he's with you in spirit. I know he is. Looking down on you today and smiling."

Emma swallowed. That thought made it even worse. Because today, marrying Cesare, she was doing something her heart told her was wrong. Doing something that her heart told her could only ultimately end in disaster, no matter how good their intentions might be for their son.

It's too late to back out, she told herself. *There's nothing I can do now.*

Irene looked at the watch on her slender wrist.

"It's time," she said cheerfully. She picked up Sam, who was wearing a baby tuxedo in his strictly honorary capacity of ring bearer. "We'll be sitting in the front row. Cheering for you both. And probably crying buckets." She waved a linen handkerchief. "But I came prepared!" She tucked it in her chiffon sash. "See you in the chapel."

"Wait." Emma swallowed, feeling suddenly panicky. She held out her arms. "I need Sam with me."

Irene looked bemused. "You want to walk up the aisle holding a baby?"

"Yes. Because—" she grasped at straws "—we're a family."

"But your hands are full…."

Emma instantly dropped the bouquet on the floor in a splash of petals, and stretched out her hands desperately. She needed to feel her baby in her arms. She needed to remind herself what she was doing this for—marrying a man who was forever in love with his dead wife. His *real* wife. She needed to feel that she was sacrificing her life for a good reason. "Give him to me."

"Aw, your poor flowers," Irene sighed, looking

at the bouquet on the floor. Then, looking up, she slowly nodded. "But maybe you're right. Maybe this is better. Here you go."

Emma took Sam in her arms. She felt the warmth of his small body and inhaled his sweet baby smell, and nearly cried.

Turning away, Irene paused at the door of Emma's bedroom. "The three of you are already a family," she said softly, "but today makes it official. Thanks for inviting me. Seeing what's possible…it makes me more happy than you'll ever know."

And her young friend left, leaving Emma holding her baby against her beaded silk dress, her throat aching as she fought back tears that had nothing to do with joy.

"All right, Sam. I guess we can't be late." She looked out the window, at the vast sky above the lake, already turning red in the twilight. "I only wish I had a sign," she murmured over the lump in her throat. "I wish I knew whether I'm making the right choice—or ruining all our lives."

Sam, of course, didn't answer, at least not in words she could understand. Holding her baby close, she walked out of her bedroom as an unmarried woman for the last time. When next she returned, she would be the mistress of this villa. From now on, her place would be in Cesare's bed.

Until he grew tired of her. And started sleeping elsewhere. She pushed the thought aside.

Emma's white satin shoes trembled as she walked down the sweeping stairs. The villa was strangely silent. Everyone had gone to the chapel, even the household staff. She heard the echoing footsteps of her shoes against the marble floor before she pushed open the enormous oak door and went outside.

Holding her baby close, she walked down the path carved into the hillside, along the edge of the lake. "This marriage is for you, Sam," she whispered. "I can live without your father loving me. I can live without him being faithful to me. For you, I can live the rest of my life with a numb, lonely heart…."

Emma stopped in front of the medieval chapel, which was lit by torchlight on the edge of the lake. Such a romantic setting. And every drop of romance a lie.

Trembling, she walked toward it, nestling

her baby against her hip as the veil trailed behind them.

The twelfth-century chapel had been carefully and lovingly restored to its Romanesque glory. The medieval walls were thick, with just a few tiny windows. The arched door was open.

Heart pounding, she stepped inside.

The dark chapel was illuminated by candlelight, its tall brass candlesticks placed along the aisle. She heard the soft music of a lute, accompanied by guitar. As she appeared in the doorway, there was an audible gasp as the people packed into the tiny chairs rose to their feet.

Emma's legs felt like jelly. She felt a tug on her translucent silk veil and saw Sam had grabbed it in his pudgy fist, and was now attempting to chew it. She smiled through her tears, then took a deep breath as the music changed to the traditional wedding march.

Looking at all the faces of the guests, she didn't recognize any of them as she slowly walked forward, feeling more dizzy with every step. She tried to focus on Cesare at the end of the aisle. She took another step, then another. She was six steps from the altar.

And then she saw his face.

Cesare looked green, sick with fear—as if only sheer will kept him from rushing straight past her in a panic. He tried to give her a smile.

Her footsteps stopped.

"Stop! Don't do it! Don't ruin your life!"

The man's voice was a low roar, as if from the deepest reaches of the earth, coming up through the stone floor. For an instant, Emma couldn't breathe. Her father's voice from beyond the grave...? Then she saw Cesare glare at someone behind her.

Whirling around, she saw Alain.

The slim salt-and-pepper-haired Frenchman took another step into the chapel. "Don't do this," he pleaded. "Falconeri has already caused the death of one woman I loved. I won't let him take another."

There was a gasp and growl across the crowd. Cesare gave a low hiss of fury. He was going to come down and smash Alain's face for doing this, she realized.

For stopping a wedding that Emma never should have agreed to in the first place.

"Don't marry him." Alain held out a trembling hand to her. "Come with me now."

She'd wanted a sign?

With tortured eyes, she turned back to Cesare. "I can't do this," she choked out. "I'm sorry."

Cradling her baby, she picked up the hem of her cream-colored silk gown with one hand, and followed Alain out of the chapel. She ran from Cesare as if the happiness of her whole life—and not just hers, but Sam's and Cesare's—depended on it.

Which she finally knew—*it did.*

As a thirteen-year-old, coming home in a strange big city, Cesare had once been mugged for the five dollars in his pocket. He'd been kicked in the gut with steel-toed boots.

This felt worse.

As if in a dream, Cesare had watched Emma walk up the aisle of the chapel, a bride more beautiful than he'd ever imagined, with their child in her arms. Then, like a sudden deadly storm, Alain Bouchard had appeared like an avenging angel. Emma had looked between the two men.

Cesare had been confident in her loyalty. He'd

known she would spurn Bouchard, and marry him as she'd promised.

Instead she'd turned on him.

She'd *abandoned* him.

For a moment, as the chapel door banged closed behind her, Cesare couldn't breathe. The pain was so intense he staggered from it.

The chapel was suddenly so quiet that he could hear the soft wind blow across the lake. The deepening shadows of the candlelit chapel seemed relentlessly dark as endless eyes focused on him, in varying degrees of shock, sympathy and worst of all—pity.

The priest, who'd met with them several times over the past weeks, spoke to him in Italian, in a low, shocked voice. He could barely hear.

Cesare's tuxedo tie was suddenly too tight around his throat. He couldn't let himself show his feelings. He couldn't even let himself *feel* them.

Emma had left him.

At the altar.

With Bouchard.

And taken their child with her.

He looked at the faces of his friends and business acquaintances, including the white-robed, hard-eyed sheikh of Makhtar in the back row, who alone had no expression of sympathy on his face. Cesare parted his lips to speak, but his throat was too tight. After all, what was there to say?

Emma had betrayed him.

Ripping off his black tie, he tossed it on the stone floor and strode grimly out of the chapel in pursuit of her.

So much for mercy. So much for the high road.

He never should have listened to old Morty Ainsley. Cesare's throat was burning, and so were his eyes. He should have sued Emma for full custody from the moment he learned of Sam's existence. He should have gotten his revenge. Gotten his war.

Instead he'd offered her everything. His throat hurt. His name. His fortune. His fidelity. Hadn't he made it clear that if she wished it, he would remain true to her? Hadn't he proven it with more than words—with his absolute faithfulness over the past year? How much more clear could he be?

And Emma had spurned all of it. In the most humiliating way possible. He'd never thought she could be so cruel. Making love to him last night—today, leaving him for another man.

He pushed through a grove of lemon trees. He would make her pay. He would make her regret. He would make her…

His heart was breaking.

He loved her.

The realization struck him like a blow, and he stopped. He loved her? He'd tried not to. Told himself he wouldn't. But all this time, he'd been lying to himself. To both of them. He'd been in love with her for a long time, possibly as long as she'd loved him.

He'd certainly been in love with her the night they'd conceived Sam. It wouldn't have made sense for him to have taken such a risk otherwise.

His body had already known what his brain and heart refused to see: he loved her. For reasons that had nothing to do with her housekeeping skills, or even now her skills as a mother, or her skills in bed. He didn't love her for any skills at all, but for the woman she was inside: loving, warm, with a heart of sunlight and fire.

And now, all that light and fire had abruptly been ripped out of his life, the moment he'd started to count on her. He wasn't even surprised. He'd known this would happen. Known the moment he let himself love again, she would disappear.

He had only himself to blame....

"Thank God you saw sense." Hearing the low rasp of Alain Bouchard's voice, Cesare ducked behind a thicket of orange trees. Peering through the branches, he saw two figures standing on the shore, frosted silver by moonlight. "Here." Bouchard's accented voice was exultant. "Get in my boat. You've made the right choice. I won't let him hurt you now."

Clenching his fists, Cesare took a step toward them. Then he saw Emma wasn't making a move to get in the boat. She had turned away, and was trying to calm the baby, who had started to whimper in her arms. Her long white veil trailed her like a ghost in moonlight.

"He didn't hurt your sister, Alain," she said in a low voice. "He would never hurt her. He loved her. In fact, he's still in love with her. That's why I...why I couldn't go through with it."

Cesare stopped, his eyes wide, and a branch broke loudly beneath his feet. Bouchard twisted his head blindly, then turned back to Emma. "Hurry. He might come at any moment."

"I'm not getting in the boat."

The Frenchman laughed. "Of course you are."

"No." Emma didn't move. "You have to accept it. Cesare is always brutally honest, even when it causes pain. Her death was a tragic accident. He's never gotten over it. Cesare is a good man. Honorable to his core."

Bouchard took a step closer to her on the moonlit shore.

"If you really believe that," he said, "what are you doing out here?"

Cesare strained to hear, not daring to breathe. He saw Emma tilt up her head.

"I love him. That's why I couldn't marry him."

Cesare stifled a gasp. She loved him?

Bouchard stared at her, then shook his head. "That doesn't make any sense, *chérie*."

She gave a low laugh. "It actually does." She wiped her eyes. "He'll never love anyone but Angélique. Heaven help me, I might have married him anyway, except…except I saw his face in the chapel," she whispered. "And I couldn't do it."

Cesare took a deep breath and stepped out of

the thicket of trees. Both figures looked back at him, startled.

"What did you see?" he asked quietly.

"Falconeri!" Bouchard stepped between them. "You might have fooled Emma, with her innocent heart. But we both know my sister's death was no accident."

"No."

"So you admit it!"

"It's time you knew the truth," Cesare said in a low voice. "I've kept it from you for too long."

"To hide your guilty conscience—"

"To protect you."

Bouchard snorted derisively. "*Protect* me."

"When she married me, she didn't want a partner. She wanted a lapdog." Cesare set his jaw. "When I threw myself into work, trying to be worthy of her, she hated the loss of attention. She hated it even more when I started to succeed. Once I no longer spent my days at her feet, worshipping her every moment, Angélique was restless. She cheated on me. Not just once, but many times. And I put up with it."

"What?" Emma gasped.

Bouchard shook his head with a snarl. "I don't believe you!"

"Her last lover was an Argentinean man she met while visiting Paris, who frequently traveled to New York on business. She decided Menendez was the answer to the emptiness in her heart."

Bouchard started. "Menendez? Raoul Menendez?"

"You know him?"

"I met him once, as he was having a late dinner in a hotel in Paris with my sister," he said uneasily. "She swore they were just old friends."

Cesare's lips curved. "Their affair lasted a year."

He frowned. "That's why she wanted a divorce?" For the first time, he sounded uncertain. "Not because you cheated on her?"

"I never could have done that," he said wearily. "I thought marriage meant forever. I thought we were in love." He turned to Emma and whispered, "Back then, I didn't know the difference between lust and love."

Emma caught her breath, her eyes luminous in the moonlight.

Bouchard stood between them, his thin face

drawn. "She called me, the night before she died—sobbing that her only love had betrayed her, abandoning her like trash, that he'd been sleeping with someone else all the while. I thought she meant you. I never thought…"

Cesare shook his head. "She wore me down over that year, demanding a divorce so she could marry Menendez. She hated me, accusing me of being her jailor—of wanting our marriage to last longer just so I'd get more of her fortune. Do you know what it's like? To live with someone who despises you, who blames you for destroying her only happiness?"

"Yes," Emma whispered, and he remembered her stepmother. His heart twisted at the pain in her beautiful face. He wanted to take her in his arms and tell her she'd never feel that kind of grief again. Trembling, he took a step toward her.

"So you let her go," Bouchard said.

"I finally set her free so she could marry him," Cesare said. "She ran off to Argentina, only to discover Menendez already had a wife there. She came back to New York broken. I'm still not sure if she was trying to kill herself—or if she was just trying to make herself go to sleep to forget the heartbreak...."

Bouchard paced, then stopped, clawing back his hair. He looked at Cesare. "If this is true, why did you never tell me? Why did you let me go on believing you were at fault—that you were to blame?"

"Because you loved your sister," he said quietly. "I didn't want you to know the truth. That kind of blind love and faith is too rare in this world."

"I insulted you, practically accused you of..." He stopped. "How could you not have thrown the truth in my face?"

Cesare shook his head. "I thought I loved her once. And I had my faults, too. Perhaps if I hadn't worked so much..."

"Are you kidding?" Emma demanded incredulously, juggling their baby against the hip of her wedding gown. He smiled.

"I'm telling you now because you both deserve to know the truth." He looked at Emma. "I didn't want anyone to know my weakness, or the real reason I never wanted to marry again. I thought love was just delusion, that led to pain." He paused. "Until I fell in love with you..."

Emma's lips parted in a soft gasp.

The Frenchman tilted his head, looking thoughtfully between them. "I think it's time for me to go." Stepping forward, he held out his hand. "*Merci,* Cesare. I have changed my mind about you. You are—not so bad. You must not be, for a woman like Emma to love you." Turning back, he kissed her softly on the cheek and gave her one final look. "*Adieu, ma chérie.* Be happy."

Climbing into his small boat, Alain Bouchard turned on the engine and drove back across the lake.

Cesare turned to face Emma. As he looked down at her beautiful stricken face, so haunted and young beneath the long white veil as she held his child, her eyes were green and shadowed as the forest around them. His heart was pounding.

"You left me at the altar," he said.

She swallowed. "Yes. I guess I did."

"You said you saw something in my face that drove you away," he said in a low voice. "What did you see?"

Moonlight caressed her beautiful face. She took a deep breath.

"Dread," she whispered. "I saw dread." Her

voice caught. "I couldn't marry a man with a face like that. No matter how much I was in love with you. I couldn't trap you into a loveless marriage for the rest of your life. And pretend not to notice as you—cheated on me, again and again."

"Cheated on you?" he demanded.

The baby started to whimper. Comforting him, she nodded miserably. "I assumed—"

"No." Going to her, he grabbed her shoulders and looked down at her. "Now you know the story, you have to know I would never betray you."

"I thought you still loved your wife," she whispered. "That I had no chance of holding your heart—"

"I was too proud to tell you the truth. I never wanted to appear vulnerable, or feel weak like that ever again. I did love her. I loved my parents, too. And all I learned was that when you love anyone—they leave."

"Oh, Cesare." Her eyes glimmered in the moonlight as she shook her head. "I'm so sorry…"

"I swore I'd never let anyone that close to me again." His lips lifted at the edges as he looked down at her. "Then I met you. And it was like coming home."

"You never said…"

"I told myself you meant nothing to me. That I'd only brought you from the hotel to be my housekeeper. But I think it was for you that I bought that house. Even then, some part of me wanted to settle down with you. With you, I lowered my guard as I never did with anyone else. And when I found you crying that night in the kitchen, it broke through me," he said hoarsely. "When I finally took you in my arms, I took everything I'd ever wanted and more…." He looked at Sam, then back at her fiercely. "Do you think it was an accident that I took such a risk? I've long since realized that my body and my heart must have known what my brain spent years trying to deny."

"What?" she whispered.

He looked down at her. "That you are for me. My true love. My only love."

She was crying openly now. "I never stopped loving you—"

He stopped her with a finger to her lips.

"I nearly died when I saw you leave with him,"

he said in a low voice. "It was like all my worst fears coming true."

"I'm sorry," she choked out. "When he broke into our wedding, I thought it was a sign, the only way to save us both from a life of misery—"

"Won't you shut up, even for a minute?" Since his finger wasn't working, he lowered his head and covered her mouth with his own. He felt her intake of breath, felt her surprise. He kissed her in the moonlight, embracing her with deep tenderness and adoration. Her lips were sweet and soft like heaven. When he finally pulled away, his voice was hoarse.

"All this time, I was afraid of loving anyone again. Because I didn't think I could handle the devastation of losing them. But I think I've always been in love with you, Emma." Reaching out, he cupped her face. "From the day we first met. And I told you that you looked smart. And that I was glad you came into my life."

A little squeak came out of her lips.

"Do you think I really came to Paris for some deal over a hotel? No." He searched her gaze. "I was looking for you. When I found out about the baby, I asked you to marry me. Then I slept with you. I did all the things I swore I'd never do. I kept breaking my own rules again and again. Over you."

"What are you saying?" she whispered.

He looked down at her in the moonlight, caressing her cheeks, running the pads of his thumbs over her pink full lips.

"Where you are concerned, from now on there is only one rule." He smiled, and her image seemed to shimmer as he said hoarsely, "I'm going to love you for the rest of my life."

"You—you really love me," she breathed.

He saw the incredulity in her eyes, the desperate hope. He thought of her years of devotion going far beyond that of any paid employee. Thought of how she'd always been by his side. How she'd always had the strength and dignity to stand up for what was right. Even today.

Especially today.

"You've shown me what love can be," he whispered. "Love isn't delusion, it isn't trying to avoid grief and pain, but holding your hand right through it, while you hold mine." He took her hand, cradling it in his own. "All this time," he said in a low voice, running his other hand along her pale translucent veil, "I was afraid of loving someone and losing them. I turned it into a self-fulfilling prophecy."

She swallowed, shifting Sam's weight against her shoulder. "It still could happen. I could get sick again. I could get hit by a bus."

"Or you could stop loving me. You could leave me for another man."

"Never," she cried, then suddenly blushed, looking down at her wedding gown. "Er, except for just now, I mean. And I didn't leave you for Alain, I never thought of him that way."

"I know."

"I couldn't marry a man who didn't love me. Because I've realized it's love that makes a family. Not promises."

Slowly Cesare lowered himself to one knee, as he should have done from the beginning. "Then let me love you for the rest of our lives. However long or short those lives might be." Taking her hands in his own, he fervently kissed each palm, then pressed them against his tuxedo jacket, over his chest. "Marry me, Emma. And whatever your answer might be, know that you hold my heart. For the rest of my life."

"As you hold mine," she said as tears ran down her face. Moving her hands, she cupped his face. And nodded.

"Yes?" he breathed, searching her gaze. "You'll marry me?"

"Yes," she said, smiling through her tears.

"Now," he demanded.

She snorted. "So bossy," she said with a laugh. "Some things never change." Her expression grew serious. "But some things do. I want to marry the man I love. The man who loves me." Her eyes grew suddenly shadowed as she shook her head. "And if anything ever happens to us…"

"We're all going to die someday." Cesare's eyes were suspiciously blurry as he looked down at her. Beneath her veil, several pins had fallen out of her chignon, causing her lustrous hair to tumble wildly down her shoulders. He pulled out the rest, tangling his fingers in her hair. "The only real question is if we're ever going to live. And from now on, my darling," he whispered as he lowered his lips to hers, "we are."

"Emma!"

"We're over here!" she called, but she knew

Cesare wouldn't be able to see her in the villa's garden. It was August, and everything was in bloom, the fruit trees, the vegetables, even the corn. She tried to stand up, but being over eight months pregnant, it wasn't easy. She had to push herself up off the ground with her hands, and then bend around in a way that made Sam, now fifteen months old and digging in the dirt beside her with his little spade, giggle as he watched her flop around.

"Mama," he laughed, yanking a flower out of the ground.

"Fine, go ahead and laugh," she said affectionately, smiling down at him. "I did this for you, too, you know."

"Fow-a." With dark, serious eyes, he handed her the flower. Every day, he looked more like Cesare, she thought. But he'd also started to remind her of her own father, Sam's namesake. She saw that in the toddler's loving eyes, in his sweetly encouraging spirit.

"Emma!" Cesare called again, more desperately.

"Over here!" She waved her hands over the

bushes, trying to make him see her. "By the orange grove!"

The garden had been transformed. Just like her life. The gold-digging supermodels of London would have been shocked and dismayed to learn that, as a billionaire's wife, Emma now spent most of her days right here, with a dirty child, growing fruits and vegetables for their kitchen and beautiful flowers to fill the vases of their home. Except, of course, when they had to fly down to the coast and go yachting along the Mediterranean, or take the private jet to see friends in London or New York. It was nice to do such things. But nicer still, she thought, to come back to their home.

The wedding had been even better than she'd imagined. After their breathless declaration and kiss by the lake, she and Cesare had gone back to the chapel arm in arm—only to discover their guests had already given up on them and started to mill back to the villa to gossip about them over some well-deserved limoncello. Even Irene looked as if she'd almost given up hope.

They'd called them all back to the chapel, and with some small, blushing explanation, the wedding had gone forward as planned. Right up to their first married kiss, which had been so passionate that it made all the guests burst into applause, and made Emma's toes curl as she'd thought she heard angels sing. The priest had been forced to clear his throat and gently remind them the honeymoon hadn't quite started yet.

She exhaled. They were a family now. They were happy. Cesare still had his international empire, but he'd cut back on travel a bit. Especially since they'd found out she was pregnant again.

"Cara." Cesare came into the clearing of the garden and took her in his arms for a long, delicious kiss. Then he knelt by their son, who was still playing in the dirt, and tousled his dark hair. "And did you have a good day, *piccino?*"

Watching the two of them, father and son, tears rose in Emma's eyes. Slowly she looked over the beauty of the garden. The summer trees were thick and green, and she could see the roof of the Falconeri villa against the bright blue Italian sky. How happy her parents would be if they could see how her life had turned out. Cesare's parents, too. She could feel their love, every time she looked at Cesare. Every time she looked at their son.

And soon, their daughter would join them. Emma's hand ran over her huge belly. In just a few weeks, their precious daughter would be born. They had already picked her name: Elena Margaret, after her two grandmothers.

Emma felt the baby kick inside her, and smiled, putting both hands over her belly now. "You like that, do you?" she murmured, then turned her face back to the sun.

"What happened while I was gone today?" Cesare rose to his feet, a frown on his handsome face. "You are crying."

Smiling, she shook her head, even as she felt tears streak down her cheeks.

Reaching out, he rubbed them away. "What is it?" he said anxiously. "Not some problem with the baby? With you?"

"No." The pregnancy had been easy. She'd been healthy all the way through, in spite of Cesare's worry. All her checkups had put her in the clear. She was safely in remission, had been for over a decade, and all her life was ahead of her. "I can't explain. I'm just so—happy."

"I'm happy, too," he whispered, putting his arms around her. He gave a sudden wicked grin. "And I'll be even happier, after Sam is tucked in bed…"

She saw what he was thinking about, in the sly seduction of his smile, and smacked him playfully on the bottom. "I'm eight months pregnant!"

"You've never been more beautiful."

"Right," she said doubtfully.

"Cara." He cupped her face. "It's true."

He kissed her until she believed him, until she felt dazed, dazzled in this garden of flowers and joy. She knew they would live here for the rest of their lives. If they were lucky, they'd someday be surrounded by a half-dozen noisy children, all splashing in the lake, sliding up and down the marble hallways in their socks, screaming and laughing like banshees. She and Cesare would be the calm center of the storm. The heart of their home.

He pulled her against him, and they stood silently in the garden, watching their son play. She heard the wind through the leaves. She exhaled.

She'd gotten everything she'd ever wanted. A man who loved her, whom she loved in return. Marriage. A snug little villa. As she felt the warmth of the sun, and listened to the cheerful chatter of their son, she leaned into her husband's embrace and thought about all the love that had existed for the generations before them. Their parents. Their parents' parents. And the love that would now exist for generations to come.

We're all going to die someday, her husband had once said. Emma realized he was wrong.

As long as love continued, life continued. Love had made them what they were. It had created Emma, and created Cesare. It had created Sam, and soon, their daughter. Love was what lasted. Love triumphed over death.

And anyone who truly loved, and was loved in return, would always live on—in this endlessly beautiful world.

* * * * *

Mills & Boon® Large Print

March 2014

MILLION DOLLAR CHRISTMAS PROPOSAL
Lucy Monroe

A DANGEROUS SOLACE
Lucy Ellis

THE CONSEQUENCES OF THAT NIGHT
Jennie Lucas

SECRETS OF A POWERFUL MAN
Chantelle Shaw

NEVER GAMBLE WITH A CAFFARELLI
Melanie Milburne

VISCONTI'S FORGOTTEN HEIR
Elizabeth Power

A TOUCH OF TEMPTATION
Tara Pammi

A LITTLE BIT OF HOLIDAY MAGIC
Melissa McClone

A CADENCE CREEK CHRISTMAS
Donna Alward

HIS UNTIL MIDNIGHT
Nikki Logan

THE ONE SHE WAS WARNED ABOUT
Shoma Narayanan

Mills & Boon® Large Print

April 2014

DEFIANT IN THE DESERT
Sharon Kendrick

NOT JUST THE BOSS'S PLAYTHING
Caitlin Crews

RUMOURS ON THE RED CARPET
Carole Mortimer

THE CHANGE IN DI NAVARRA'S PLAN
Lynn Raye Harris

THE PRINCE SHE NEVER KNEW
Kate Hewitt

HIS ULTIMATE PRIZE
Maya Blake

MORE THAN A CONVENIENT MARRIAGE?
Dani Collins

SECOND CHANCE WITH HER SOLDIER
Barbara Hannay

SNOWED IN WITH THE BILLIONAIRE
Caroline Anderson

CHRISTMAS AT THE CASTLE
Marion Lennox

BEWARE OF THE BOSS
Leah Ashton

0314 Rom LP

Discover more romance at

www.millsandboon.co.uk

- ❤ WIN great prizes in our exclusive competitions
- ❤ BUY new titles before they hit the shops
- ❤ BROWSE new books and REVIEW your favourites
- ❤ SAVE on new books with the Mills & Boon® Bookclub™
- ❤ DISCOVER new authors

PLUS, to chat about your favourite reads, get the latest news and find special offers:

- ❤ Find us on facebook.com/millsandboon
- ❤ Follow us on twitter.com/millsandboonuk
- ❤ Sign up to our newsletter at millsandboon.co.uk